DEFENDERS OF SAME-SEX COURTSHIP

Volume One

Gracefully written by Mr. Abdul Robinson

"I am a selfless orphan. I've been taught the art of storytelling by a headless swordsman."

--Abdul Robinson

Abdul Robinson

"Famine and misfortune to those that shun and oppose same-sex marriage..."

--Shammar Scott

DEDICATION

This book is dedicated to those that respect the law of INDIVIDUALITY.

This book is dedicated to those that sincerely support same-sex courtship,

Same-sex wooing,

Same-sex marriage,

Same-sex adoption,

Same-sex parenting,

Same-sex nuptials and

Same-sex lovemaking...

--Abdul Robinson

DEDICATION

A brief moment of silence for those that that were lost in the phone to be recognized.

This book is dedicated to the gay community and every advocate that's in unwavering alliance with the LGBT family.

This book is dedicated to the entities that love the phrase EQUALITY.

--Shammar Scott

Due to the innovative and influential subject matter, viewer discretion is sincerely advised...

--Shammar Scott

Due to the iniquitous, egregious and woeful subject matter, viewer discretion is definitely advised...

--Abdul Robinson

This is a novel of savage conflict and enduring faith...

... Keeps the reader hanging on every word and provides encouragement for these last days. Quite simply, I doubt there has ever been a work of LGBT fiction to compare to *Defenders of Same-Sex Courtship*...

--Anonymous

ACKNOWLEDGEMENTS

I would like to acknowledge the assistance of Shammar Scott and Deandre Robinson, the friendship of Eric Henderson, and the expertise of the eloquent voice in my head. None of them are responsible for points of view or errors contained in this story. Much of the locale, most of the events, and all of the characters in this story are fictional.

To begin, I would like to thank God, who has always provided such critical support at critical times, and who, far more than anyone else, allowed me to complete the novel on schedule. Though I might dedicate a thousand books to the Lord, I could never truly show my heartfelt gratitude for his selfless assistance, both in this and in countless other moments of my life. Some debts are simply too great to be repaid. To continue, I would like to thank the voice in my head for its unshakable courage, its unwavering support and friendship, and for standing solidly behind me during those crucial hours. I thank the voice within for freely providing its genius, its vision, and a generous number of its INCOMPARABLE ideas to greatly enhance the storyline and characters. In retrospect I realize, more than ever before, that this novel was no simple task. Capturing the world inhabited by America's most elite Same-Sex Defenders while at the same time portraying a compelling moral story was by far the most difficult fictional challenge I have ever faced.

God bless my two sons... NARRU R. HERRON and PRINCE ABDUL R. ROBINSON.

--Abdul Robinson

PRAISE

"Among the greatest works of imaginative fiction of the twenty-first century."
--Deandre Robinson

"One of the great fairytale quests in modern literature."
--Shammar Scott

"A work of immense narrative power that can sweep the reader up and hold him enthralled for days and weeks."
--Anonymous

"This story takes place against a background of measureless depth... That background is ever-present in the creator's mind, and it gives Carla and company a three-dimensional reality that is seldom found in this kind of writing."
--Eric Henderson

"A masterful story... An epic in its own way... with elements of high adventure, suspense, mystery, poetry and fantasy."

"It illustrates the ultimate battle between homosexuals and heterosexuals, a grim, tragic, brooding and beautiful book, shot through with heroism and hope..."

"Its power is almost that of mysticism."

--Anonymous

CHAPTER ONE— LGBT

As I allowed my whiskey-colored Rolls Royce Phantom to pompously parallel park itself, I thought about the one man that makes me feel special and relevant...

Thoughts about my soon-to-be husband were rudely neutralized the moment I spotted an aspiring mobster, dressed to the hilt in Ferragamo apparel, clutching a poorly manufactured picket sign. The anti-gay insignia that was printed on the picket sign not only ruffled my feathers, but it also sent chills up my spine, me being the openly gay man that I am. I covertly exited the Phantom.

After exiting my chariot, I adjusted my corset and slyly adjusted my shoulder holster. After adjusting my shoulder holster, I abruptly removed my Gianvito Rossi peep toe pumps and sashayed over to the hypocritical hoodlum clutching the picket sign...

It took me a little over thirteen seconds to get within striking range...

Once within striking range, I immediately snatched the picket sign from the judgmental jackass and broke the sign into three different fragments... Before he had the luxury of assessing the situation, I delivered a well-choreographed kick to his sternum...

The fact that he started coughing up blood and mucus seconds after the kick was delivered was irrefutable evidence that I had either ruptured his spleen or cracked his thorax.

I wasn't surprised to see the culprit then fall to the pavement. As he hit the pavement I noticed that his eyes were hazel-colored, and his Ferragamo moccasins were scruffy and out of season... Semi-satisfied with the volatile neutralization of one of the pipsqueak picketers, I diverted my attention to another male dressed to the nines in Dolce and Gabbanna apparel. It took everything in me not to extract the .38 revolver from my suede shoulder holster and put several dime-size holes in his trachea.

I incautiously approached the male protester. I could smell the fear seeping out of his pores as I closed the gap between us. The picket sign he was foolishly clutching had the despicable phrase "FAGGOT" painted in bold capital letters across the anterior of the placard... Unbeknownst to the picketer, I was just conveying to my fiancé that the son of a bitch that integrated the phrase faggot into the planet's regional variety of spoken language needs to be castrated and placed in a sixteenth century guillotine... My boo agreed that the word faggot needs to be obliterated from civilization's entire language dialogue...

After giving the protester a direct order to hand over the picket sign, I could hear the obnoxious sound of police sirens in the distance.

Just as the tasteless boycotter made a sincere effort to comply with the direct order I gave him, I head-butted the loser... He hit the pavement like a sack of redskin potatoes.

The teeth marks on my forehead, along with the fact that he was now screaming like a damsel in distress, were solid indicators that his palate was compromised indefinitely and he'd most likely spend the remainder of his existence wearing dentures...

After adjusting my eight hundred dollar wig and glaring at several other protestors, I nonchalantly swaggered over to my awaiting armored Phantom. After retrieving my designer pumps form the curb, I slithered into the Rolls Royce.

Once seated in the driver's seat, I pushed one of the eighty-eight buttons that peppered the dash panel and the Phantom sneezed to life. The digitized dashboard gracefully lit up. Seconds later, I diplomatically integrated the Phantom into oncoming traffic... The two police cruisers that zipped past me with their sirens blaring and their multicolored lights flashing were surely en route to gather information from the two injured protesters and the slew of onlookers...

Thirty-eight minutes later I was giving my openly gay butler stern instructions to park the Rolls Royce around back next to the 1934 Duesenberg. I then entered my chateau and made a beeline to my vanity station, so I could assess the magnitude of the teeth indentations that were now in the center of my forehead. Shortly after scrutinizing the indentations, I was convinced that his incisors made the imprint and that the EMTs were combing the pavement in search of his four front teeth that, once upon a time, rested between his canines...

"What the fuck happened to you?" asked Walter as he emerged from my walk-in closet, wearing nothing but a pair of flamingo-colored boy shorts and a pair of Manolo Blahnik slippers...

The scowl on my face alerted Walter that I was in no mood to be questioned and in no mood to brief him on the meritorious mayhem that I sagaciously carried out...

Walter was my most trusted admiral. Although he had the slutty disposition of a promiscuous burlesque dancer and the vernacular of a video vixen, he understood me, he understood men and he understood our lifestyle. And most importantly, he properly understood the laws and bylaws of INDIVIDUALITY.

Walter was what I like to call a bisexual brute that found comfort in protecting drag queens... He has the physique of a straw weight MMA fighter and the mystique of a Hollywood harlot...

I met Walter several summers ago in South Beach at a glamorous bistro called Pump. He complimented my Alexander McQueen turtleneck and my Patricia von Musulin necklace... And before I knew it, we were buying one another cocktails. After purchasing a case of muscatel for my openly gay comrades, I ended up telling Walter that I was actually a former NFL quarterback dressed in ladylike garments. I gave him minor details about my attraction to men and my aspirations of someday undergoing a series of surgeries so I will be able to possess big boobs, a slender torso and a vaginal cavity that's able to discharge fluids and of course coquettishly constrict...

After briefing Walter about my sexual preference, he confided in me about his romantic liaisons with elite men and college students... Several weeks later I offered him a top-ranking position in a dynasty I was astutely assembling, entitled the DEFENDERS OF SAME-SEX COURTSHIP.

To my surprise, Walter quickly showed a keen interest in the movement... Several days later he was sworn in, illicitly deputized and officially knighted.

After a three-month-long probationary period, I finally introduced Walter to the four cofounders of our dynasty−

Of course all four of the cofounders were openly gay and proud to be gay.

The four cofounders consisted of two young ladies that only dated ladies and two elderly men that were engaged to be married to one another...

All six of us shared this eight-bedroom estate...

Kevin and Devin were probably in the theatre room watching reruns of the Ellen DeGeneres Show.

After putting two small Band-Aids over the teeth imprints, I entered the den and wasn't shocked to discover Heather and Sharon fully nude, smoking hand-rolled cigars.

Heather and Sharon were been being bullied as adolescents, both were motherless and fatherless, and both had years ago pledged their allegiance to me, the LGBT community, and the equality coalition that I ingeniously founded, organized, endowed and set up...

"Where's Kevin?" I asked while noticing that both dames were in need of a Brazilian wax and a French pedicure...

"Kevin's in the conference room, preparing our weekend itinerary," stated Heather after blowing a barrage of smoke rings into the air...

"What the hell happened to your forehead?" asked Sharon as she swiped foreign dust particles off of my Azede suede peacoat...

"Quiet as kept, I crossed paths with an imbecile brandishing a picket sign that had the phrase FAGGOT painted on the placard, so I made an executive decision to head-butt the creep... And of course the head-butt sufficed at seeing to it that the creep will spend the next thirty-eight days or so ingesting vittles through a straw..."

"I believe the head-butt to the mouth was a bit egregious," shouted Heather as she straightened my high-priced wig...

"Don't be absurd," stated Sharon. "If the asshole had the audacity to be brandishing a placard that had the word FAGGOT written on it, then the man was clearly looking for trouble and clearly identifying himself as an evil enemy of the gay community... Therefore, our commander-in-chief dealt with the prick accordingly..."

"What's up ladies?" shouted Devin as he stormed into the den, clutching his iPad... His breath smelled of butterscotch candy...

"Where's Kevin?" I asked after playfully squeezing Devin's butt...

"He's in the conference room, chatting online with a British lad that resembles the dashing and dauntless Anderson Cooper... He mentioned that the British industrialist has ties to the LGBT community and that he's sincerely interested in becoming one of the Defenders of Same-Sex Courtship..."

"Has Kevin been able to adequately tally the number of openly gay followers that have been following us and our risqué regime on Facebook, Twitter and Instagram?" asked Heather as she blew another half dozen smoke rings into the air...

"Be advised Commander, our openly gay number of Twitter followers is at one million and climbing. The number of closeted followers that have been faithfully following our movement and us on Facebook continues to climb; yet it also frequently fluctuates. It's at three million. The heterosexual followers that have been visiting our websites and liking us on Instagram has just peaked at six million... There's a grand total of eight million emails that I've yet to review. The amount of hate mail that's been pouring in from all over the country is incalculable, and the footage of you fiendishly injuring two harmless heterosexual protestors has just been uploaded to the Internet... Anti-Gay Advocates has labeled your volatile actions as being graceless and tasteless."

CHAPTER TWO— LESBIANS

"Does anyone have any trustworthy intel on these glamorous Defenders of Same-Sex Courtship?" asked Detective Stevenson after reviewing the teeth fragments that were recovered at the crime scene...

"I've got several attaché cases crammed with reliable intelligence about the founder, the four cofounders and their eighty-six volatile constituents," stated Detective Sanders after extracting a glazed donut from the box that sat atop their unmarked police cruiser...

"So what's the story with these eighty-six volatile constituents?" asked Detective Stevenson as he watched several paramedics place one of the injured protestors onto a stretcher...

"Six or so confidential informants that were reliable in the past tell me that the Defenders of Same-Sex Courtship have a total of eighty-six shrewd sentinels that promote and facilitate the evolutionary process of same-sex marriage... All eighty-six sentinels are rumored to be gay, bisexual, transsexual, transgendered, etc. etc. Sources further confirmed that all eighty-six sentinels are combat savvy and flamboyantly voguish..."

"Why hasn't The Department followed up on these leads?" asked Detective Stevenson as several protestors marched past, shouting anti-gay remarks...

"It's a touchy assignment," stated Detective Sanders. "No one wants to criminally pursue a rogue regiment of LGBT affiliates. It's considered treasonous and taboo to target openly gay citizens in the manner with which we target urban youth and solution-oriented immigrants."

"Were you ever able to obtain video and audio footage of the founder and cofounders of this gay gang?" asked Detective Stevenson as he helped himself to a jelly donut.

"FYI, Sir... They're not a gang, they're an international entity that has a ravenous compulsion to stage gay pride parades every other week and ruin those that are lobbying against gay rights and same-sex adoption... And for the record, Sir, I've obtained some shoddy footage of the four cofounders. It's been very difficult to obtain photos and footage of the infamous founder of this bisexual bureaucracy."

"I'd like to review the footage you've obtained of the four cofounders, and I want to launch a covert investigation against the Defenders of Same-Sex Courtship," shouted Detective Stevenson after tossing his half-eaten jelly donut to an ebony-colored Persian cat that circled their squad car...

"We're homicide detectives," stated Detective Sanders. "We've been deputized to solve senseless killings and apprehend murderers... We'll be the laughingstock of The Force if we haul in the founder of a gay movement and eighty-six of her homosexual henchmen."

"Do you have any data on the identity of the founder that gave birth to this cabinet of queens and queers?"

"The gender of the founder has yet to be established," stated Detective Sanders as he adjusted the channel frequency on his wireless portable walkie-talkie. "Several of my informants conveyed to me that the founder is a white male, early thirties, blue eyes, five foot nine... one hundred eighty pounds... blond hair, German accent and plenty of capital...A few of my other informants mentioned that the founder is a blue-eyed damsel that's utterly attractive, five foot eight... one hundred seventy pounds, raven-colored hair, Jamaican accent, late twenties with an acute sense of fashion... Goes by the name of Carla when she's in an evening gown and goes by the name Karl when he's dressed in Tom Ford suits and Nike apparel."

"So the founder is a cross-dresser?" asked Stevenson as he climbed into the unmarked cruiser.

"No, Sir... The founder is an openly gay patriarch that's in the process of metamorphosing into a munificent matriarch."

"Were your informants able to give you an address for their headquarters?"

"Their headquarters is a huge convention center called The Pink House. It has a one-hundred-seventy-five-person state-of-the-art conference theater with tiered seating and a fully interactive A/V setup... The Internet bloggers mentioned that their lair sits on approximately four hundred acres, and has 1.3 million square feet of total exhibit space. Two arenas with flexible layouts – Freedom Hall holds over nineteen thousand people and Broadbent Arena holds six thousand six hundred people."

"How do you know all of this shit?" asked Stevenson after glancing down at his Brera Orologi timepiece.

"If you google "The Pink House," it'll tell you how their same-sex fortress has over seven hundred fifty thousand total square feet of prime exhibit space – all on ground level, plus fifty-four flexible meeting rooms from five hundred ninety square feet to twenty-five thousand square feet, wifi, virtual private networks, broadband Internet, VoIP and analog phone technology..."

"I've heard enough about The Pink House," shouted Stevenson. "I'd like to hear information about the racketeering rumors that these homosexuals are allegedly involved in. I'd like to know what makes these Defenders of Same-Sex Courtship think they're untouchable and so lovable... I'd like to know which one of these homosexuals thought it would be admirable and gallant to kick a lacrosse coach in the sternum and head-butt a heterosexual hipster... I'd like to know why our prissy mayor hasn't had these glamorous pirates formally indicted under the RICO act..."

"The mayor is a proud supporter of the LGBT community," stated Sanders after retrieving a pair of dual speed loaders from the glove compartment. "The mayor also understands that that if he criminally pursues the founder and cofounders of the Defenders of Same-Sex Courtship, he'd more than likely wake up chained to a gynecologist's chair with his mouth and rectum skillfully stapled shut as a Vietnamese lesbian manually inserts maggots doused in venom that's been methodically extracted from an Asian pit viper down his urethra."

"Don't be so dramatic," shouted Stevenson as he adjusted the rearview mirror.

"I'm not being dramatic," shouted Sanders. "I'd rather challenge the Sinaloa cartel than taunt the Defenders of Same-Sex Courtship. The last federal agent to accuse the Defenders of money laundering, extortion and tax evasion mysteriously ended up being kidnapped, hog-tied, anesthetized and administered a full sex change."

"Urban legends about flagrant fags are synthetic tales that were manufactured by Hollywood socialites to defer homophobic debutantes from judging those that are transgendered and attracted to the opposite sex..."

"I'd sincerely appreciate it if you didn't use the term fag when referring to the gay citizens of this country," stated Detective Sanders after putting on his Tom Ford sunglasses. "The term fag is a word that the tongue should be restricted from pronouncing..."

"You sound like a groveling gay advocate that's not in favor of eradicating the Same-Sex Marriage Bill!" shouted Stevenson while making an illegal U-turn at a busy intersection.

"I sound like a man that respects the laws of INDIVIDUALITY," shouted Sanders. "I sound like a man of integrity and humility. I sound like a man that properly understands the ramifications for showing hate towards openly gay civilians in the twenty-first century, a malicious transgression that the gods frown upon, an infraction that's never awarded amnesty..."

"Blah, blah, blah," shouted Stevenson while parking behind a pistachio-colored Porsche 911.

"We're homicide detectives," stated Sanders. "Let's investigate homicides and not squander our time setting snares for influential homosexuals that are simply in the pursuit of love, romance and EQUALITY."

"I've become disenchanted with capturing young black men and charging them with capital murder," stated Stevenson after retrieving a quarter bag of heroin from the front pocket of his Nautica trousers. "I now have this compulsion to lock up every queer in this metropolis that's encouraging and sponsoring same-sex adoption, same-sex spooning, same-sex courting, same-sex lovemaking... same-sex newlyweds and same-sex nuptials..."

"Keep your voice down," whispered Sanders, "because if the Defenders receive intelligence that you're making dishonorable statements about their lifestyle, changes are you'll be found unconscious, crammed in a chicken coop with your tongue nailed to the roof of your mouth."

"Fuck the Defenders of Same-Sex Courtship," shouted Detective Stevenson as he poured a small amount of heroin onto one of his debit cards, "and fuck the pompous politicians that refuse to veto the Same-Sex Marriage Bill... And since you're all for equality, I guess it's fuck you, too," shouted Stevenson right before he snorted the evil powder.

Detective Sanders glared at Stevenson as he prepared another line of heroin for himself...

"Hey, take it easy with that shit," shouted Sanders after Stevenson swiftly snorted the second line of heroin.

"Listen here, Dipshit," shouted Stevenson as he poured another small portion of heroin onto the debit card. "When it comes to manhandling this here heroin and setting snares for sissies, I don't need any wise counsel. You just worry about solving homicides and sending young black boys to prison for the rest of their lives, since that's your primary obsession and your fruitless forte."

"Fuck you!" yelled Sanders. "And just so you know, I hate locking black men up, I hate patrolling these poverty-stricken neighborhoods, targeting these fatherless fathers that are in truth defeated by their circumstances. You're a bigger idiot than I thought if you're under the impression that it excites me to rob these urban men of their freedom."

"I've been your partner for a little over ten months now, and during the course of these ten months I can testify under oath that you've arrested at least thirty-eight hundred African American boys and saw to it that two thousand of those black boys went to prison," stated Stevenson after snorting another line of the sinister powder. "Now, if I'm not mistaken, you've been a cop for almost five years now so I'm guessing you've participated in at least thirty thousand arrests that involved inner-city men of color. So how dare you judge me for deciding to criminally pursue homosexuals, when at the end of the day, you're an African American male that would rather use your time and the Department's resources to tackle colored boys and haul them off to one of the slew of maximum security prisons located in southern Illinois than assist me with the formidable mission of ridding this city of the salacious gay men, women and teenagers that are attempting to construct legacies."

Unbeknownst to Detective Stevenson, Sanders had been covertly recording their entire conversation via wireless bug that was secretly affixed to the Kevlar vest he had on underneath his Armani cable knit designer cardigan...

As Stevenson snorted the last of his personal batch of heroin, Sanders was scheming on how to get the recorded conversation to his fiancée Carla before Kevin revised their weekend itineraries.

CHAPTER THREE— GAY

Kevin exited the conference room, confident that Carla would be pleased with this weekend's itinerary. The redolence of Estée Lauder oil sheen assured Kevin that the commander-in-chief was either in the den with the twins or in the foyer boasting to their bashful butler about how she'd soon be MRS. SANDERS and how next week her hubby would submit his resignation notice to abort the field of law enforcement...

As Kevin approached the door that led into the den, he could clearly hear the twins snickering and Carla chuckling...

Kevin entered the den and rushed over to the twins, pinched their tushies. After playfully squeezing their apple-shaped derrieres, he saluted Devin and marched over to Carla.

"What's up, playboy?" shouted Carla as Kevin planted two soft dry kisses on the Band-Aids that cloaked the teeth imprints.

"I'm exhausted, babe," stated Kevin as Heather knelt down and began appraising the leather ankle holsters that encircled his left and right ankle. "I've been doing some extensive research on the number of openly gay Persians (Iranians) that reside in the United States. I've also spent the entire afternoon tallying the number of nationalities that are gradually becoming respectful and receptive to the LGBT lifestyle."

"Is that a new tattoo on your forearm?" asked Carla as she pointed at Kevin's right arm.

"It's a day or so old," stated Sharon as she playfully blew smoke rings in Kevin's direction.

"Would the commander-in-chief like to scrutinize the artistry?" asked Devin after swiftly grabbing Kevin's right wrist.

"I'm sure you'll fancy the tattoo and marvel at the artistry," shouted Heather.

"It's a grand portrait of DON LEMON," shouted Kevin as he hiked up his sleeve to give his commander an unobstructed view of the thirty-eight-hour-old tattoo.

"Hubba, hubba," whispered Carla while gazing at the wallet-size portrait tattoo of the devout DON LEMON.

"He's a thoughtful heartthrob," shouted Sharon.

"I'd like to count his eyelashes," shouted Devin as the twins retrieved their satin panties off the porcelain gargoyle sculpture that was positioned next to a door-size oil painting of Billy Jean King.

"The artistry is magnificent," stated Carla after saluting Kevin and winking at Devin.

"Where's Walter?" asked Kevin while adjusting his sleeve and making eye contact with Sharon as she stepped into her leather leggings.

"Walter's organizing my walk-in closet," stated Carla just as Heather wiggled into her Level 99 jeans.

"Are you prepared to verbally brief me on the details of our weekend itinerary?" asked Carla after glancing at the cuckoo clock perched atop a glass cabinet that held Elton John memorabilia and Boy George figurines.

"A digest of our itinerary has been uploaded to your Palm Pilot as you firmly requested," stated Kevin while adjusting his diamond-studded cufflinks. "Later this evening, several of our cargo planes will be stocked with vaginal cleansing products and other feminine hygienic essentials. Once the planes are fully stocked you'll be notified, and the minute you give the polyamorous aviators clearance to take flight, the healthful emergency provisions will be swiftly airlifted to SRI LANKA and RWANDA as you commanded. After the planes have touched down gracefully, the tampons, Monistat 7 creams and other vaginal medicinals will be equally rationed out to the malnourished motherless mothers that reside in those desolate villages."

"Didn't I suggest that one plane be stocked with dehydrated beans and rice, and several barrels of smoked king salmon strips?" asked Carla as she swiped foreign dust particles off the Jason Collins bobble-head doll that sat to the right of an autographed Lady Gaga CD.

"Yep... you sure did, babe," shouted Kevin. "I vividly recall you giving me firm instructions to have the beans, rice and salmon airlifted to the famished families in Haiti... Those two planes reached Haiti without incident. Several hours ago I received confirmation that the victuals were portioned out fairly."

"What about the plane I personally stocked with five-gallon buckets filled with canned sardines and mackerel?" asked Heather while Sharon fastened her strapless bra.

"That plane reached Nigeria without incident and the Nigerian adolescents were grateful and elated to receive the vittles. Oh, and as you requested babe, Sherman Hemsley's tombstone has been refurbished and revitalized. The invoice for that arrived forty minutes ago. Any minute now, I should receive confirmation from our Russian accountants that the eight hundred grand we donated to the National Amputation Foundation was wired into their account... And I'm still waiting on several checks to clear so we can donate another seventy thousand to the Arthritis Foundation, and another sixteen grand to the United Cerebral Palsy Association..."

"Has Loyd called?" asked Carla as Walter entered the den, clutching an open bottle of chilled Chardonnay.

"Aren't those my boy shorts?" asked Sharon while putting on her salmon-colored Bally boots.

"If these were your boy shorts, my ass wouldn't be spilling out of the sides," shouted Walter after rolling his eyes. "But anyway, I'm done organizing your closet, Ms. Carla. Would you like me to pour you a cocktail?"

"I'm in no mood for a cocktail. I'd like to know why the hell my fiancé hasn't called me or texted me."

"Calm down, Commander," whispered Devin. "I'm sure Mr. Sanders will be home within the hour."

"Has he told his playmates on the force that he's gay?" asked

Heather as she put on her bulletproof vest over her camo-print crop top.

"Mind your business, Heather," shouted Kevin.

"Don't yell at my sister," shouted Sharon while glaring at Kevin.

"SUSPEND the bickering!" shouted Carla as she walked over to the game room that had recently been converted into a makeshift armory.

The armory held enough weaponry to iniquitously annihilate a colony of mean-spirited homophobic bullies. Carla's weapon of choice was the bantam-size flamethrower. Therefore, the twins weren't surprised to see Carla enter the armory and make her way over to the flamethrower.

The flamethrower in question was a weapon that shoots flaming oil, napalm, etc. Etched along the muzzle of the flamethrower was the inscription, "In loving memory of Luther Vandross."

"Where are the six muskets that were given to us by Rock Hudson's former comrade?" asked Carla while seductively sliding her index finger across the stock of the flamethrower.

"They're in the trunk of the BMW i8, primed for transport," stated Devin while examining the leather Balmain jacket that rested on a shelf that was designed to hold several recoilless rifles.

"I almost forgot that we were giving the muskets to the bisexual gunsmith in exchange for three sawed-off shotguns," stated Carla as she diverted her attention to the Montblanc satchel that sat in the corner, next to a modern sporting rifle that was built in the style of the M-16.

"Why the fuck hasn't this valise been placed in the cellar with the rest of this month's spoils?" asked Carla while pointing at the Montblanc satchel.

"The twins told Kevin and Devin that you wanted to appraise the previous stones from last week's gem heist before they were hauled to the cellar," stated Walter while being sure to look Carla in her eyes as he spoke.

"Although I don't recall making such a request... someone please give me some information about the color and quality of the precious stones you all seized from the judgmental jeweler that refuses to sell engagement rings and other trinkets to same-sex couples."

"The quality of gems we seized ARE fit for queens and oil tycoons," stated Heather while placing a break-action single-barrel shotgun on its assigned rack.

"In terms of quantity, there's quite a number of emeralds and diamonds," stated Sharon. "And there's a batch of rubies and sapphires... The array of gems includes pearls, upscale solitaires, topazes that are the color of ripe banana peels, blue-green turquoises, jades, opals and garnets..."

"What sort of residual effect can we expect from a mediocre score such as this?" asked Carla while removing one of the lever-action rifles from its designated stand.

"It's obviously difficult to assume just how much the Japanese fencer will offer us for the vast amount of cute colorful gems," stated Kevin while gazing at the over/under break-action double-barreled shotgun that was horizontally mounted on the far left wall. "But if forced to give an estimate of the stolen stones... I'd say his initial offer will be a million dollars cash in small bills, which would surely suffice since we're planning to use the capital from the heist to purchase new ritzy monument markers and funerary statues for the dearly departed Rosa Parks, Harriet Tubman and Maya Angelou."

"I have no desire to appraise the gems," stated Carla. "Arrange a meeting with the lighthearted Japanese fencer. If he offers us a million dollars in small bills..., refrain from giving him a counter offer. Accept the million dollars and we'll selflessly move forward with our stratagem of upgrading the fallen damsels' headstones."

"When did we obtain these thirteen side-by-side break-action shotguns?" asked Heather as she took a selfie of herself clutching one of the shotguns.

"Be careful with that, sis," shouted Sharon. "It's loaded."

"That's a bad-ass shotgun," shouted Devin. "As you can see, it features a pair of barrels mounted beside each other. It's the homosexual's go-to gun, especially for gay men such as drag queens... Many of these shotguns are made with double triggers – one to a barrel – for an instant choice of which choke to use... And just so you know, an openly gay pawnshop owner that's attracted to me gave us the shotguns as a token of his appreciation for all the transgendered teens we've helped to combat their anxiety and depression."

"I can't seem to find the dragon skin vest that Loyd gave me last month," stated Carla, just as several masked assassins brandishing Chinese assault rifles, dressed in sleek tactical riot gear had appeared in the den.

"It's in the footlocker next to the poster of Rock Hudson," stated Heather as several assassins covertly tiptoed toward the armory.

"Who has a key to this footlocker?" asked Carla, just as the hired slayers stormed into the armory and egregiously began shooting.

Carla and her squad were mowed down before they could intelligently defend themselves...

Kevin was the first Defender to be fatally wounded. The first shot that was fired struck Kevin in his right eye, which sent him crashing into a glass gun rack. While en route to seek cover, he received multiple rounds to his upper and lower back.

Seconds before Kevin was struck in his lower and upper back, Carla was struck in the testicles. The jock strap Carla was wearing did a poor job of protecting his male reproductive glands.

At the exact same moment that Carla was struck in the crotch, the free-spirited twins were both struck in the chest.

The bullets that struck Sharon pierced her breastplate. The bulletproof vest that Heather had on over her camo-print crop top did a splendid, merciful job of protecting her mammary glands. The bullet she received seconds later woefully entered her vaginal cavity...

The twins' frantic screaming stimulated the trained assassins. As Walter was reaching for the caribou-colored carbine perched atop the copper trestle, he was immediately struck in his mouth, collar and femur. The projectile that entered his mouth granted his teeth amnesty, yet grazed his tongue, pierced his uvula and punctured his palatine tonsil. The blood that now leaked from Walter's eyes, nose and ears assured all three gunmen that the cute boy in the trendy boy shorts was now deceased.

The life-threatening injuries that Carla, Kevin and the twins received were minor compared to the catastrophic injuries that Devin was allotted during the wicked onslaught... The six or so .280 Remington shells that perforated Devin's petite physique caused Carla to scream in horror.

The masked assassins spent a little under ten seconds in the armory. A total of thirty-three rounds were fired. .280 Remington brass shell casings and .270 Winchester casings now littered the floor of the armory.

While Carla and her LGBT troops lay sprawled out on the marble floor, two of the homophobic executioners stealthily exited the armory. The last villain to exit the armory was Carla's former arch nemesis, a slutty Slovakian siren that couldn't stand gay men. Before exiting the armory, the murder-for-hire siren snatched Carla's pricey wig off of her head and seductively sashayed out of the arsenal...

CHAPTER FOUR— BISEXUAL

As I sat at my vanity station, disassembling and methodically reassembling my Gatling gun, I thought about Carla and the infamous Defenders of Same-Sex Courtship. I thought about the gay advocates that are under the foolish impression that they're called to facilitate, promote and uplift same-sex marriage. My thoughts were brought to a halt the second I noticed that the apparatus affixed to my iPad was chirping.

The chirping was clear-cut confirmation that the bitch Carla and her polyamorous housemates were silenced in the manner I requested... Six minutes later, I was wiring another seven hundred grand into Catilina's offshore account...

Catilina was a Slovakian supermodel that went rogue when she discovered that her former fiancé was having sexual relations with a cartel boss that was old enough to be her grandpa... Weeks after the betrayal, Catalina joined forced with a murder-for-hire agency that only accepted jobs that revolved around lynching lesbians, silencing sissies and castrating members of the LGBT community...

I met the villainous vixen online. He lewd profile intrigued me. After days of chatting online, she revealed to me that she hated gay men and how she's with a co-ed coven that specializes in harming homosexuals for elite, affluent heterosexuals. Several days later, partial payment and arrangements were made to have the founder or the cofounders of Same-Sex Courtship assassinated by decapitation.

After wiring the funds into Catalina's account, I poured myself a glass of Kettle One vodka and extracted a Cuban cigar from the glass cigar case stationed on the mantle above the fireplace.

"Good news, boss," I gleefully shouted just as Jessica and her two bullmastiffs entered the living room.

"You never have good news," Jessica sternly stated while removing her suede belted coat.

"I assure you, Boss Lady, I've done a deed that you'll deem worthy of a celebration."

"It's been quite a spell since you've done a deed worthy of a celebration," stated Jessica. "You've botched a slew of major heroin deals this year, you spend way too much time in those chat rooms and every time I cross paths with you, you're clutching a goblet filed with whiskey, bourbon, or vodka. So if you're in possession of some good news, I suggest you spill the beans because I have no time to hear about one of your mediocre drug deals. I've got a busy day ahead of me. In exactly three hours I've got a meeting with the founder of the Defenders of Same-Sex Courtship movement. She claims to have the capital and a stratagem to get two dozen of the fifty schools reopened that were recently unjustly closed in Chicago."

"I thought you hated her," I nervously stated as her two bullmastiffs circled me and sniffed my Oxford shoes.

"I do hate her," shouted Jessica after ingesting several prescription pills. "But the bitch is a full-blooded mastermind. She's innovative and influential. And if I've got to join forces with this he/she to accomplish what I'm trying to accomplish, then so be it. It's paramount that I infiltrate her same-sex regime so I can become her apprentice and her prominent protégé."

"The bosses in New York would be livid if they knew that your primary aspiration in life is to be a vixen under Carla's tutelage."

"Listen here, you dimwit," shouted Jessica as the female mastiff snarled at me. "I refuse to spend the rest of my life peddling heroin for the Asian cartel and trafficking firearms for the Dutch brothers. If a damsel of my caliber gets caught trafficking firearms across state lines, I'll be placed in a ten by ten cage and the District Attorney will see to it that the door to my assigned cage is welded shut."

"The bitch Carla isn't as smart as you think," I firmly stated after lighting my cigar. "I'd rather eat glass and ingest gas than seek wise counsel from a dude in a French Connection dress and Giuseppe Zanotti heels."

"With that attitude, you'll spend the remainder of your existence as a pompous pawn in pursuit of ill-gotten gains," stated Jessica after taking a seat on the footstool adjacent to my vanity station. "Carla's solution oriented and she's calculative like a Chinese emperor. It's in my best interests to befriend her so I can emulate her thought patterns and someday construct my own regime of rogue humanitarians."

"I hate to interject babe, and I hate to inform you that forty-eight hours ago I made an executive decision to have Carla and her Same-Sex Sentinels slaughtered. I received confirmation that the founder and cofounders of Same-Sex Courtship have been slayed in their own sex lair. And just so you know, a dame by the name Jessica charged us a little over a million dollars to eradicate all six Same-Sex affiliates."

"Surely you don't expect me to believe that an upscale drunk such as yourself paid a harlot a million dollars to murder Carla and her squad?"

"I swear to you boss, I had Carla and her gay compadres murdered. I just received notification that Carla and the others are officially neutralized."

"Who the fuck gave you authorization to have Carla and her pals dispatched?" asked Jessica while glaring at me. Her two mastiffs seemed aware that their owner was now upset because they gracefully sat down in front of me.

"Since when do I need authorization to behead a platoon of STD-carrying homosexuals?" I asked sarcastically after blowing cigar smoke in the face of the male mastiff.

"Let me get this straight," stated Jessica as the female mastiff began to growl and foam at the mouth. "You took it upon yourself to have the charitable Carla killed?"

"That's correct, boss," I candidly stated after blowing more smoke in the face of the mastiff.

"Before I give Bonnie and Clyde a direct order to disembowel you, it's my duty to inform you that you're a classless knight on my proverbial chessboard. You're a simple chess piece that has let me down more times than I care to count. I see you've forgotten your place; you've gotten complacent and arrogant. You sit here and tell me that you've had Carla and other Same-Sex members killed, and seconds later you sit before me and insubordinately below smoke in the face of my loyal canines?"

The scowl on Jessica's face told me that she was disenchanted with me and furious that I paid to have her idol assassinated. A small part of me didn't yet believe that she would have Bonnie and Clyde attack me. Me being the fearless gangster that I am, I intentionally blew smoke in the face of the female mastiff.

"Who's the cunt that you paid a million dollars of our money to murder Carla and her unit?" asked Jessica as she sashayed over to where my Gatling gun rested.

"She's a Slovakian hit woman that I met online," I calmly stated while trying not to make eye contact with the mastiffs.

"Give me one reason why I shouldn't allow Bonnie and Clyde to take your life," asked Jessica after glancing down at the Swiss-made SLYDE timepiece that encircled her right wrist.

"Fuck you and Carla. I quit. I'm done being your flunky and I'm done having you speak to me as if I'm a fucking junkie. I've stolen dogs twice as volatile as these cuddly guard dogs."

"Fuck me, huh?" asked Jessica as she covertly instructed the canines to assault me.

The male mastiff leapt forward and sunk his teeth into my right kneecap. I felt my patella shatter. A swift second later, the female mastiff pounced forward and sunk her canines into my left shin. I felt my tibia and fibula simultaneously shatter. As I screamed and repeatedly struck the male mastiff with a closed fist, I could hear Jessica ranting and raving about Carla's attributes, accomplishment and accolades.

Eight seconds into the dog attack I felt myself getting fatigued and lightheaded. Just as blood leaked out of my kneecap, the female mastiff released my shin and began sinking her incisors into my throat. I felt her canines puncture my windpipe and pierce my jugular region. Before completely losing consciousness, I felt more of her teeth perforate my larynx and prick my trachea.

As everything went black, I felt myself gargling blood and saliva. I knew I was perishing when I felt urine discharging from my urethra and feces discharging from my rectum...

CHAPTER FIVE— TRANSSEXUAL

Catilina and her two callous companions exited the den and made a nonchalant beeline for the front door.

While marching through the foyer, Catilina couldn't help but notice that the wooden sculpture of Jason Collins planted in the center of the foyer had blood splattered all across the face and left shoulder blade.

Sixty-eight centimeters to the right of the wooden sculpture was Carla's bisexual butler. His throat had been slit and several bones in his wrist had been broken, courtesy of Catilina and her trusty scalpel.

The three evildoers exited the front door and each slithered into their awaiting sports car.

The three camel-colored convertibles that the assassins climbed into were 2009 Ferrari 16M Spiders. As the replica Ferraris swerved out of the cobblestone driveway, Carla's fiancé Loyd was swerving onto the cobblestone driveway. Loyd found it slightly odd that three replica Ferraris were fleeing the premises.

The sole fact that all three Ferraris were the same color and exact make and model assured Loyd that their visit to Carla's estate was business related and LGBT-oriented. After parking behind Heather's 2008 Lamborghini Murcielago, Loyd exited his sedan and casually entered their love nest.

He was greeted by the flagrant odor of blood and gunpowder. The iniquitous scent of gunpowder and blood swiftly swayed Loyd to extract the .45 from his hip holster.

Just as Loyd was cocking back the hammer of the .45, he spotted the butler laying face down in a pool of his own blood and urine. Loyd spent the next forty seconds or so incautiously going from room to room, searching for his queen and her amorous admirals.

"Carla..." shouted Loyd as he entered the music room. The music room was empty.

"Carla," yelled Loyd as he entered the boardroom... After discovering that the boardroom was empty, Loyd entered and exited the conference room, the study, the library, the master bedroom and the cellar...

"Carla..." shouted Loyd as he entered the den. The conspicuous scent of blood and gunpowder was prevalent in the den.

Shortly after charging into the den, Loyd spotted Carla sprawled out in the threshold of their makeshift armory.

"Carla," shouted Loyd as he raced over to revive her.

"Carla!" screamed Loyd as he checked for a pulse.

Once confirmation was established that Carla was alive, Loyd assessed the massacre. The savage and indiscriminate wholesale killing made Loyd's eyes water.

Seconds later, Loyd was giving a female fire and rescue dispatcher a gruesome verbal synopsis of the murder scene. Immediately after giving the dispatcher the address, he suspended the call and knelt before Carla as if he was getting knighted.

"I'll find the monsters that did this to you and your friends," whispered Loyd as he realized Carla was struck in the groin region. "Don't die on me, baby," whispered Loyd as he protectively lay down next to Carla and wrapped his arms around her.

While spooning with Carla in a large puddle of her own blood, Loyd surveyed the five corpses that were sprawled out on the floor of the armory...

He couldn't help but notice that Devin's injuries were twice as harsh as the twins' injuries. Loyd properly understood that Devin and Kevin were deceased. The image of the three Ferraris crossed Loyd's mind as he glared at the bullet hole in Kevin's right eye socket.

Loyd was utterly certain that the monsters that carried out this slaying were astute, acute and abominable.

Loyd spent the next thirty seconds conveying to a male fire and rescue dispatcher that he was certain that the agile assailants were traveling northbound in brown-on-brown identical Ferraris. After giving the 911 dispatcher a direct order to put a 3.8.9 alert out on three sand-colored Ferraris last seen traveling northbound, he terminated the call with the dispatcher and kissed Carla on her forehead. As the sound of fire truck horns and ambulance sirens could be heard approaching their estate, Loyd began counting Carla's eyelashes.

Out of his left peripheral he spotted Walter. The fecal matter that soiled the trendy boy shorts he was wearing was a grim indicator that Walter died a little over three minutes ago...

As Loyd spotted Heather, he noticed that she was wearing a bulletproof vest over her crop top. The blood that was profusely leaking from her vaginal region alerted Loyd that the stunning Heather was struck in the uterus...

The high-caliber Remington shell cartridges that littered the armory floor along with the Winchester shell casings were sound evidence that the villains that orchestrated the obliteration of his precious pals were professional operatives that were killers by trade. As Loyd counted Carla's mink eyelashes for the fourth time, approximately eight unmarked police cruisers swerved onto their cobblestone driveway, along with six marked squad cars...

As the homicide detectives exited their vehicles, a Channel 6 news chopper could be heard and seen hovering overhead. As the uniformed cops climbed out of their US flag-colored police cruisers, fleets of news vans were parking along the perimeter of the premises.

As the news vans were selecting promising vantage points, two fire trucks and eight EMT vans swerved onto the cobblestone driveway, followed by three meat wagons, two coroner carriages, two forensic lorries and an armored tactical caravan that was assigned to and designed for the police commissioner...

The moment the two coroners exited their carriages they started giving several uniformed officers the green light to line the perimeter with yellow and red tape...

"Any positive ID on the victims?" asked the commissioner after quickly exiting his armored caravan.

"Detective Sanders has confirmed that there are a total of seven victims... two females, five males," shouted one of the coroners while adjusting his reading glasses. "All seven victims were severely injured... Six via gunshot wounds from high-caliber hunting rifles. One victim has his throat slit from ear to ear..."

"Any survivors?" asked the commissioner as he and the two coroners crossed the threshold of the home.

"We've been instructed that there's possibly five fatalities and two possible survivors," stated the coroner while putting on a pair of latex surgical gloves. "As for identification, we have no concrete ID on six of the victims but we're confident that one of the victims, and most likely the primary target, is Karl Sims, the selfless founder of an eccentric regime entitled the Defenders of Same-Sex Courtship..."

CHAPTER SIX— EQUALITY

EIGHT HOURS LATER, EIGHT MILES AWAY FROM CARLA'S ESTATE...

I entered my villa clutching a bantam-size rocket launcher and a silk pillowcase filled with high-quality sex toys...

After entering my villa, I was greeted by my new boyfriend. We spend thirteen seconds or so smooching in the foyer. I suspended the make-out session the second I noticed that we BOTH had full-fledged erections... The vixen within wanted to give him the dick suck of his life, but I understood that he wasn't worthy quite yet of a monumental blowjob...

After respectfully suspending the smooching session, I swaggered into the guestroom and placed the rocket launcher next to a French horn that I plan to someday give to Michael Sam. With the rocket launcher now secured in the guestroom, I reentered the foyer and wasn't surprised to see that my boyfriend Josh was now stark naked... His nine-inch penis stood at attention. My tonsils twitched at the thought of deep-throating his sword... I felt my own dick re-stiffen as I appraised his physique and mystique.

Unbeknownst to Josh, I had already decided that tonight would be the night I'd let him enter me and sample my goodies.

Several hours ago I had wisely decided that I wouldn't award him with one of my infamous dick sucks until he'd been evaluated and appraised by my commander-in-chief, Carla. Josh was a selfless scoundrel that was well-aware that I was one of the top-ranking officials for the Defenders of Same-Sex Courtship, yet he wasn't aware that Carla always advised her LGBT cohorts to never orally please someone unless that person is special and worthy in all aspects.

As Josh seductively marched toward me with his dick in his left hand and a white rose in his right hand, my mouth watered and I felt a droplet of pre-cum drip from my urethra...

I placed the pillowcase filled with sex toys in a yellow hamper that was filled with George Michael records... Seconds later, Josh was kneeling before me as if he was about to propose.

I gazed into Josh's eyes and I could see love and lust harmoniously coexisting within his dilated pupils.

Josh handed me the cotton-colored rose and frantically began clawing at my Gucci belt buckle. As I held the rose under my nose to smell its pollination orifice, Josh had managed to salaciously unfasten my belt buckle and uncinch the metal button affixed to my Fendi trousers...

Before I could thank Josh for the rose, I heard the sound of my zipper being manually retracted. The distinct sound of my zipper being manipulated stimulated me in such a way that I did the honors of pulling my own dick out so Josh could have his way with it...

As I coquettishly unveiled my ten-inch ebony-colored python, I allowed Josh to pull my trousers and Polo boxer briefs down to my ankles.

While clutching my manhood with both hands, I slyly stepped out of my boxer briefs and Fendi trousers. I released my python to unbutton my long-sleeved flannel.

The very second I removed my hands; Josh began planting wet kisses across the shaft and tip of my penis. My python uncontrollably pulsated as Josh skillfully caressed my inner thigh...

"Thanks for the rose, babe," I seductively whispered just as I slowly inserted my dick into his welcoming mouth.

My toes abruptly began to curl and wiggle as I felt the tip of my penis repeatedly kiss his palatine tonsil. The inside of his mouth was warm, slimy and watery...

Josh and I gazed into each other's eyes as he crammed every inch of me inside his mouth. Just as I felt the tip of my dick kiss his tonsils for the fiftieth time in thirty-eight seconds, I felt the digitized bracelet that encircled my left wrist vibrate.

A quick glance at the diminutive posh screen disclosed that my commander-in-chief had been woefully wounded and airlifted to a prominent, providential ER surgery center. Three seconds later I was prying Josh's mouth and talons from around my sword.

"What's wrong, sweetie?" asked Josh as I stepped back into my boxer briefs and linen trousers.

"Carla's been shot," I sorrowfully shouted while fastening my slacks and adjusting my designer belt. "I'll be back in a couple of days," I sternly stated before reentering the guestroom to retrieve my rocket launcher.

Now armed with the rocket launcher, I exited the guestroom, kissed Josh on the tip of his nose, raced out of my luxurious villa, and climbed into my pumpkin-colored Audi R8. After turning the ignition key counter-clockwise and pressing several buttons on the gadget clasped around my wrist, the R8 hissed to life and the voice of Sherman Hemsley came streaming out of the Clarion speakers that were mounted inside the driver and passenger door panels.

The retractable twenty-two-inch plasma monitor that was mounted in the center of the dash panel chirped melodiously as I placed the rocket launcher on the passenger seat.

Just as intelligence about Carla's portion of misfortune came into focus on the monitor, I began crying. Tears of anguish and grief cascaded down my cheeks and soiled my silk tank top. Without wiping my tears, I slammed the gearshift into fourth and stomped on the accelerator pedal. The R8 rocketed into the rush hour traffic. The high-pitched screech from the puncture-proof radial tires startled my neighbor and his twelve-year-old son.

While traveling east doing a little over eighty-six miles per hour, I decided that I would stop by The Pink House before I vengefully butchered the first heterosexual couple I encountered.

As one of the elite Defenders of Same-Sex Courtship, I knew that LGBT protocol warrants that I report to The Pink House, converse with other high-ranking cohorts, connect the dots, identify the hypocritical captious culprit, strategically draft a preliminary stratagem to covertly apprehend the culprit, his companions, his comrades and his concubines, and deal with the pompous participating parties in a manner that's taboo and vile...

After running several red lights I wiped the tears from my eyes and glared at the retractable monitor. The classified intel that was composed on the plasma screen confirmed that some highly trained heterosexual operatives ambushed Carla, Heather, Sharon and Walter, as well as Kevin and Devin. Also posted was a cryptic message printed in Swahili...

The message was stern and precise... It stated that all vindictive, villainous and volatile Defenders of Same-Sex Courtship were to promptly meet at The Pink House dressed in flamingo-colored fatigues, armed with one's weapon of choice, and emotionally prepared to declare war against those that despise EQUALITY and same-sex marriage.

CHAPTER SEVEN— TRANSGENDERED

"Where to, ladies?" asked Janet and Jackie's German chauffeur as he climbed behind the wheel of their elk-colored Escalade ESV E-1...

"The Museum of Science and Industry," shouted Jackie as she hiked up her Gabbana gown to alert Janet that her silk panties were crotch less.

As the Escalade began traveling north on the Dan Ryan Expressway, Janet began inserting several of her fingers inside of Jackie's wet pussy... Seconds later the priceless aroma of fresh adult pussy filled the air of the SUV... The German chauffeur glanced up at his rearview mirror and wasn't at all surprised to see that Jackie had her designer gown hiked up over her waist with her legs spread wide open. As Janet dexterously slid her fingers in and out of Jackie's love tunnel, the chauffeur got hot and bothered as he heard the sexual whimpering and heavy breathing coming from the cabin of the E-1...

Janet spent the next two and a half minutes playing with Jackie's pussy...

Over the course of those hot two minutes, Jackie had already leaked and squirted approximately a teaspoon of slimy whitish fluid onto the leather jump seats. The nosy driver gazed up at his rearview mirror for the thirtieth time and was elated to discover that Janet had teasingly postponed the finger-pleasing foreplay and began hoggishly swiping her tongue across Jackie's constricting clitoris...

"Yes..." shouted Jackie as she felt Janet's tongue taunting her voracious vulva.

Jackie's dramatic whimpering inspired Janet to haphazardly plant small hickeys around her vaginal cavity. The hickey-planting pussy-eating session went on for a pleasant six minutes. Jacked had climaxed twice and yanked out strands of her own hair extensions during the two climactic orgasms...

Unbeknownst to the chauffeur and Jackie, Janet's panties were now damp. The perspiration and steam that was emanating from her own palpitating pussy had soiled her satin panties. Jackie, being the keen lover that she is, sensed that Janet's vaginal region was twitching and itching for some oral attention.

"I love you," whispered Jackie as she used her left hand to hike up Janet's Lacoste skirt...

With Janet's skirt now hiked up over her waist, Jackie used her right index finger along with her middle finger to slide Janet's wet panties eight centimeters to the left. The intoxicating redolence of female urine fused with Summer's Eve vaginal cleanser greeted Jackie as she shoved her tongue deep inside of Janet's love box.

Janet scratched and clawed at the wood grain and leather that cloaked the plush seats and posh door panels as Jackie's tongue danced inside of her womb. Janet's whimpering aroused the German chauffeur, although he was only attracted to male athletes.

The windows in the Escalade began to fog up as Janet gyrated her hips and justly squirted warm cum into Jackie's mouth...

Jackie diverted her tongue to Janet's now swollen clitoris.

Janet squealed and squirmed as Jackie's tongue and fingers poked and swiped at her clitoris.

Just as Jackie blew hot air at Janet's pussy, the digitized contraption clamped around her left ankle began chirping sporadically. Seconds later the gadget clasped around the chauffeur's left wrist began chiming. As the driver glared at the wrist device, the sleek apparatus that encircled Janet's right ankle began beeping and vibrating.

"Carla's been shot," shouted the German chauffeur while pulling into a Wal-Mart parking lot. "She's been airlifted to a prestigious infirmary."

As the driver pulled into the Wal-Mart parking lot, Janet and Jackie found it hard to believe that their life-alert anklets were chiming and vibrating. Both women thoroughly understood that the devices were specifically designed to alert the Defenders of Same-Sex Courtship that the commander-in-chief was apprehended or injured...

After Janet gave the driver stern instructions to usher them to The Pink House, Jackie was extracting a .90 shot Uzi from her Rebecca Minkoff tote bag.

As the driver pulled out of the Wal-Mart parking lot, he glanced over at the bazooka stationed on the passenger seat while gazing at the baby Uzi Jackie had just pulled from her tote bag.

Janet cautiously pulled eight Korean hand grenades from her suede Fossil bag and placed them on her lap.

A minute or so after Jackie, Janet and the German chauffeur were alerted about Carla's misfortune, approximately thirty-eight hundred LGBT affiliates were simultaneously notified. Out of the thirty-eight hundred affiliates, eighty-six were deputized Defenders of the Same-Sex Courtship Infantry. These eighty-six openly gay sentinels were literally the muscle of the gay community. All eighty-six were prima donnas that enjoyed bullying the bullies that bullied bisexual bachelors.

All eighty-six were affluent and entitled. Each was a homeowner and gun owner. The most voguish and volatile out of the eighty-six affiliates was an African American female gunsmith, age thirty-four. She's attracted to women, yet doesn't mind playing with a stiff dick every now and then. The minute she heard about Carla being shot in her own chateau, she retrieved her sniper rifle from her wine cellar and her pink fatigues from the attic... Eight minutes later she was en route to The Pink House.

The first Same-Sex operative to reach The Pink House was Daisy. She entered The Pink House clutching a Roman two-headed battle-axe. The scowl on her face was a sure indication that she was in the mood to scalp a heterosexual hypocrite.

Next to arrive at The Pink House was Nolan, an openly gay gangster that was wanted in six different states. The Scandinavian gangster exited his V13R Roadster and entered The Pink House. The Tommy gun he was feloniously clutching was fully loaded.

Just as Nolan crossed the threshold, Nate and Tasha were climbing out of their two-door Maserati. Nate and Tasha were both transgendered and both comfortable with the idea of starting a sex war with those that shunned EQUIALITY. The two compound bows that Nate was carrying were a telltale sign that he had no problem killing in the name of Same-Sex Courtship. The Desert Eagle in Tasha's right hand and the Desert Eagle lounging in the hip holster affixed to her left hip were confirmation that, if given orders to slay a judgmental jackass, she'd respond accordingly.

Minutes after Nate and Tasha entered The Pink House, Tina and thirteen drag queens exited a fleet of armored tactical and riot trucks. All thirteen of the drag queens were crying, all were clutching sleek samurai swords; all were wearing Nine West sandals and expensive wigs. The bayonet that Tina was brandishing was a detachable blade that could be put on the muzzle of the rifle that was concealed under her Mango trench coat.

As Tina and the drag queens marched into The Pink House, three armored buses and eight armored SUVs pulled in front of the building. Forty-six openly gay snipers exited one of the buses and quickly began positioning themselves around the outer perimeter of The Pink House. The sniper rifles that each sniper was militarily clutching were outfitted with high-definition scopes and German suppressors. The six-inch silencers were what gave the rifles their ominous appearance...

Thirty-three lesbians exited the second armored bus. All thirty-three damsels were dressed in neon-pink fatigues and snow-colored Jean-Michel Cazabat booties. The submachine guns that each dame carried were black and slightly compact. The women filed out of the bus with scowls on their faces. They too wasted no time positioning themselves around the outer perimeter of The Pink House...

The sixteen bisexual brutes that stormed out of the third armored bus were dressed in pink fatigues as well. Over their pink fatigues, the brutes were cloaked in full Kevlar body armor. US diplomats had the M-16s that they were cradling provided to them. They secretly and frequently indulged in sexual liaisons with LGBT affiliates.

The sixteen bisexuals, cloaked in full body armor, sashayed over to the entrance of The Pink House and stood guard outside the entry. Their squad was vigilant and competent in regards to making sure that only openly gay martyrs entered their sovereign command center.

The eight pink-on-pink modified SUVs had Red Cross emblems and Cancer Awareness emblems painted on their hoods. The eight drivers were in no mood to negotiate with the terrorist group that was behind the assassination attempt on their charitable commander-in-chief. The eight voluptuous Defenders gracefully slithered out of the armored SUVs and made a beeline for the front entrance. Unbeknownst to Carla and the dearly departed cofounders, the eight Defenders recently had the phrase TRANSJUSTICE tattooed across their foreheads. The AK-47s that each was toting were utter verification that their role in the gay community was to protect and serve...

As the eight Defenders entered The Pink House, a plethora of cars, truck and armored vans pulled into the parking port adjacent to The Pink House. The young men and young ladies that nimbly climbed out of the luxury sedans were armed with sawed-off shotguns and canisters of tear gas.

The gay goons that crawled out of the snazzy trucks and armored vans were armed as well... The semiautomatic rifles they possessed were imported from Spain. The tears in many of their eyes were tears of anger.

They all marched into The Pink House after saluting the sixteen bisexuals cloaked in full body armor. The small army entered The Pink House and was elated to discover that the foyer and lobby were teeming with hostile homosexuals in possession of their weapons of choice. At the moment there were a little over eight hundred openly gay executioners inside The Pink House and several hundred more positioned outside the perimeter of The Pink House. Each executioner was primed to administer capital punishment to all heterosexual haters that identified themselves as enemies of LGBT...

Openly gay men and women from all walks of life were en route to The Pink House. Many had no idea that a sex war may ensue...

By the time Loyd had entered The Pink House, there were approximately twenty-six hundred armed, amorous, agitated affiliates seated and standing in the spacious auditorium. Four hundred eighty-seven gay men were in the foyer, oiling their weapons and conversing about potential targets. Seventy-three polyamorous snipers were stationed on the rooftop of The Pink House, hoping that war against the hateful heterosexuals was officially decreed and justly declared.

The transgendered supermodels that were assigned to guard the rear entrance of The Pink House were lusting to injure those that viewed gay people as the scum of the earth. The three hundred seventy-six drag queens that were standing in the parking port all glared at Detective Stevenson as he parked his unmarked police cruiser behind a mustard-colored Bentley GT. The shit-eating grin on his face caused a dozen drag queens to unholster their weapon...

CHAPTER EIGHT— HOMOSEXUALITY

I swaggered into The Pink House with tears in my eyes and a scowl on my face. The bantam-size rocket launcher was appraised by many of my heartbroken comrades as I marched through the foyer. The portable weapon I was clutching was used for launching armor-piercing rockets.

Several hundred lighthearted gangsters and I sashayed into the auditorium.

"There have to be at least two thousand openly gay Defenders in this auditorium," I thought as I made my way to the elevated podium. As I approached the podium, the protectors of the gay community awarded me with their silence and undivided attention.

Me being second in command, I was obligated to brief the battalion on the iniquitous travesty that occurred at Carla's chateau... I was also morally obligated to now declare war on those that despise same-sex parents...

"Good evening, brothers and sisters," I mournfully shouted while adjusting the wireless microphone. "For those of you that don't know who I am, my name is Sebastian Turner. I'm the second in command. I'm a devout pioneer of this syndicate that Carla and the others sagaciously assembled...

"Before I bring everyone up to speed on today's calamity, let's first have a brief moment of silence for our founder and cofounders." After the forty-second memorial silence, I sat my rocket launcher on the pink footstool that was stationed on the left of the microphone stand.

"FYI, ladies and gentlemen, today approximately eight hours ago evil visited our commander-in-chief and our four cofounders... I received sincere intelligence from Carla's fiancé that three masked intruders entered Carla's home undetected... Seconds after entering the estate, the butler was ambushed and skillfully assassinated – his throat was slit from ear to ear. After maliciously neutralizing the butler, the three malevolent maniacs covertly combed the chateau and ultimately ambushed Carla and our cofounders inside their arsenal chamber.

"It kills me to inform the multitude that Carla was immediately airlifted to an honorable hospital. She's in critical condition. Several EMTs have confirmed that she was struck in the penis. She's now in surgery. The sound surgeons are confident that she'll survive and recover. As for our two patriarchs, Kevin and Devin, both men were pronounced dead the moment the paramedics checked their vitals. Also pronounced dead on the scene was one of Carla's trusted admirals. His name was Walter."

"Are the twins okay?" shouted a drag queen dressed in Mathieu Mirano, clutching a two-edged fencing sword.

"The twins were both egregiously injured. Sharon was killed during the onslaught. Heather was struck in the chest and vaginal region. The vest she was wearing protected her upper body, but the round that punctured her vaginal cavity did some extensive and gruesome tissue damage. The surgeons couldn't quite determine if Heather would survive or not."

"Walter's a former lover of mine," shouted a fellow toting a brass pitchfork. "Do you have any intel on his injuries?"

"As I've said before, Walter was pronounced dead on the scene. His injuries were brutal – he was shot multiple times. One bullet struck him in the collar, another bullet hit him in the mouth... and if I'm not mistaken, he was struck in his right femur."

"Who's responsible for this iniquity?" asked a transgendered lad cradling a Tech-9, dressed in Azede Jean-Pierre apparel.

"We've yet to receive any reliable intel on who orchestrated the attack and who actually carried out the attack. However, I did have the luxury of conversing with Carla's fiancé on the matter. He's a homicide detective. His name is Loyd Sanders. He was the first on the scene. He conveyed to me that, as he swerved onto Carla's cobblestone driveway, he spotted three tan Ferraris leaving the premises..."

"He didn't find it odd that three tan Ferraris were pulling out of the driveway just as he was pulling into the driveway?" asked Joanne, a distraught damsel brandishing a flamethrower.

"YES, I indeed found it odd," shouted Detective Sanders as he made his way to the podium.

Everyone in attendance, including myself, gawked at Loyd as he strutted across the platform and stepped in front of the microphone.

"Good evening, members and Defenders of Same-Sex Courtship. My name is Detective Loyd Sanders. I'm Carla's faithful fiancé. Although I've yet to go public with the fact that I'm attracted to men, I'm in alliance with three hundred eighty-three gay advocates, and my lifestyle is in alignment with Same-Sex Courtship. I love Carla and I'm in love with all that's cohesive with Same-Sex Courtship. As of today, I will profess and proclaim to the Law Enforcement Bureau that I'm a gay man.

"Now that I'm officially out of the fucking closet, I'd like to give you all an accurate description of the make and model of the three Ferraris. The exotic sports cars were deer-colored. Each had chrome wheels and radial tires. All three vehicles were topless convertibles, 2009 Ferraris, 16M Spiders, each in mint condition. I was able to catch a glimpse of one of the license plates.

"After discovering the bodies of Carla and the others, I ran the plate numbers through the Department's DMV database, which revealed that all three vessels were purchased from a five-star dealer that's connected to the DuPont Registry dot com. After breaking eight of the dealer's ten fingers, he admitted to leasing all three convertibles to a Slovakian damsel by the name of Catilina Ortega.

"A former lover of mine that works for the Central Intelligence Agency ran the name Catilina Ortega through their international database. CIA records revealed that Catilina is a Slovakian madam that's wanted in France for sex trafficking and grand larceny. The operative assigned to the case mentioned that Catilina has a history of participating in murder-for-hire jobs. Several APBs have been sent out on the three Ferraris. The GPS and OnStar systems in all three sports cars have been removed. The vehicles were last seen traveling east on I-57."

I listened astutely as Loyd went on and on about the alleged assassins and their getaway vessels. Just as I was about to interject, I spotted several drag queens entering the auditorium, dragging a gagged detective by his breeches.

Abdul Robinson

CHAPTER NINE— DRAG QUEENS

Detective Stevenson climbed out of his unmarked police cruiser with his badge in his left hand and a bouquet of dead flowers in his right hand. The shit-eating grin on his face telegraphed that his objective was to mock the death of their cool cofounders and celebrate Carla's calamity.

"Hey, you punks got permits for those weapons?" asked Stevenson after he exited his cruiser.

"Hi, handsome," shouted the drag queen, clutching a musket. "Are those flowers for me?"

Before Stevenson could answer, a petite drag queen stepped forward and struck Stevenson in the liver with a standard-size sledgehammer. The blow to the liver sent Stevenson to his knees. Before Stevenson could muster the will to scream, a Persian drag queen stepped forward and crammed a pair of cotton panties into his mouth.

After shoving the panties into his mouth, another drag queen snatched the revolver out of the holster that was stationed on Stevenson's right hip.

"Handcuff the son of a bitch," shouted a drag queen dressed in pink coveralls, fishnet stockings and black combat boots.

As one stunning drag queen secured Stevenson's wrist with his own handcuffs, another very attractive drag queen retrieved the handheld walkie-talkie that was affixed to his belt.

"Relinquish that bulletproof vest," shouted a queen in peep toe pumps, clutching a sharp saber...

Seventy-two seconds after exiting his cruiser, Detective Stevenson was hog-tied, gagged and stripped down to his knickers. The cantaloupe-colored cotton panties that were jammed into his mouth muffled his screams of agony. The tears in his eyes were tears of fear fused with tears of ultra pain. The proverbial deer in the headlights look that was now etched onto his face pleased the drag queens.

As other patrol cars were swerving onto the premises, they had no idea that one of their private eyes was just seconds ago hit in the liver with a sledgehammer and dragged into The Pink House. Just as Detective Stevenson was being hauled into the auditorium, a fleet of patrol cars was lining the outer perimeter of The Pink House. A Mexican standoff was gradually forming.

The same-sex sentinels that were designated to secure the outer perimeter glared at the cops as they cautiously climbed out of their police cruisers with their weapons drawn. Many of the uniformed patrolmen didn't quite understand why hundreds of openly gay men and women were on the streets, clutching weapons and displaying a menacing parade of dauntless oneness. Several officers marveled at the homosexuals as they brandished their weapons and flaunted their homogeneousness and their sexuality. Several lieutenants gawked at scowls on the homosexuals' faces and the assault rifles they were collectively cradling.

As several sergeants radioed in for SWAT and additional tactical units, a number of foreign sedans swerved onto the premises. The Defenders that incautiously climbed out of the sedans were all armed. Six of the Defenders gave the cops the middle finger as they swaggered over to their armed amigos...

"These punks are ready for war," shouted a uniformed officer, just as a pink tour bus pulled into the parking port.

Unbeknownst to the army of cops, the tour bus was filled with openly gay teens. Many of the teens were suburban eighth graders and suburban sophomores. Eighty percent of the teens seated on the bus were armed with brass knuckles, golf clubs and homemade Molotov cocktails. As three SWAT riot trucks pulled into the parking port, the gay teenagers filed out of the tour bus, wielding Molotov cocktails, baseball bats, crowbars and other blunt objects...

The SWAT teams exited their riot trucks and were instantly befuddled and overwhelmed by the sight of the armed homosexuals.

"There's at least two thousand of them," shouted one of the SWAT officers as he retrieved a shield from the rear of the truck.

"I heard that there's another two thousand or so inside the building," shouted another SWAT officer as he glared at the hundreds of armed drag queens standing in the parking port wielding flamethrowers and machine guns.

"There's no way in hell we'll be able to neutralize this regime of fags," whispered the SWAT captain as another tour bus filled with Latino lesbians and bisexual Brazilians parked directly behind the riot trucks. The lesbians that exited the tour bus were clutching picket signs and large canisters of pepper spray. The phrase EQUALITY was printed on the majority of the placards. Every lesbian that exited the tour bus was dressed in gothic attire. Their raven-colored leather miniskirts complimented their torn fishnet stockings. The crow-colored lipstick that coated their luscious lips matched the black fingernail polish that covered their nails. A dozen of the ladies stuck out their tongues at the SWAT unit as they sashayed past them. Many of their tongues were pierced, as well as their lips and noses.

The bisexual Brazilians strutted off the tour bus in unison formation. Most of the Brazilians were overtly carrying tennis ball-size hand grenades. Quite a few of the bisexuals snarled at the members of SWAT.

"Are those real hand grenades?" asked the SWAT captain as he spotted a Trans Am parking behind a BMW i8.

Behind the wheel of the Trans Am was a transgendered tycoon that believed in homosexuality and same-sex coitus. On his lap sat a box of .357 shells. On the passenger seat of the Trans Am sat a chrome .357. Parking to the left of the Trans Am was a K-9 unit. Several uniformed officers exited the K-9 unit with their assigned deputized German shepherds. The canines exited the SUV with a chip on their shoulders. Their loud growls and frantic barking telegraphed the level of disgust they had for the sight of the armed homosexuals. A minute of so after the K-9 unit arrived on the scene, Jessica and her two mastiffs arrived. The highly trained bullmastiffs leapt out of the cab of the Silverado pickup truck.

Jessica and the mastiffs marched toward an openly gay operative clutching a recoilless rifle. Once in his immediate presence, she flashed her synthetic LGBT badge at the operative. After assessing Jessica's badge, the operative lowered his weapon and modified his disposition.

"Nice shoes," stated the operative after giving Jessica a quick peck on the cheek.

"Thanks. They're Alexander McQueens," stated Jessica as she locked eyes with one of the K-9 handlers. "How long have you all been out here?" asked Jessica as she noticed her two mastiffs zeroing in on the German shepherds that appeared eager to engage in muzzle-to-muzzle combat.

"We've been out here a little over thirty-eight minutes," stated the operative as he witnessed the two mastiffs defiantly lock eyes with several of the deputized canines. "You may want to put those hounds on a leash, babe," whispered the operative, "because those German shepherds seem ready to lock horns with your pets."

Jessica's two mastiffs glared at the K-9s. The intense glaring assured Jessica that her dogs were lusting to engage in combat with the police dogs. Without warning, Jessica snapped her fingers and the bullmastiffs charged at the K-9 unit. Both mastiffs reached their targets in a matter of seconds. The male mastiff sunk his fangs into the chest of a female German shepherd as the female mastiff sunk her teeth into the face of the male German shepherd. The two shepherds screeched and wailed as the bullmastiffs stayed committed to their bites.

CHAPTER TEN— SAME-SEX COURTING

As my senses of sight and smell were abruptly restored, I didn't quite understand why I was being transported from a hospital gurney to a stretcher on wheels... The catheter that was now being inserted into my urethra was slender and flexible. The tubes that the handsome surgeon was shoving up my nose were connected to a breathing apparatus that chirped and buzzed annoyingly every few seconds or so. While glaring at the IV that was taped to my right arm, thoughts about the attack began to flash in my mind.

"Excuse me, sir... Are my brothers and sisters alright?" I calmly asked the blue-eyed surgeon that was scribbling notes onto a portable clipboard.

"I hate to be the bearer of calamitous news... but it's my duty to inform you that Walter Jones, Sharon Simpson, and Kevin and Devin McKray all died on the scene. Your butler Michael Moore also perished on the scene. You and Heather Simpson are the only survivors."

"How many times was I shot?"

"You were struck once in the groin, Karl."

"I prefer to be called Carla," I sternly stated while fidgeting with the pulse-reading device that was taped to my index finger.

Before he could snobbishly respond, a federal agent entered the ER. The sway in her hip along with the nickel-plated handcuffs in her right hand made me uncomfortable.

"Hey, you can't just barge in here," shouted the handsome surgeon.

"Shut the fuck up and assess this queer's heart rate as I read him his Miranda rights and slap the cuffs on him," shouted the federal agent as she glared at me.

As the disrespectful agent made her way over to the stretcher that I was stretched out on, I couldn't help but notice that the sleek leather hip holster clipped to the waistline of her Stella McCartney skirt was doing a shabby job of securing the compact .380 that rested in the holster. Seconds before she officially reached the stretcher, I'd already made an executive decision to disarm the bitch and explain to her the importance of EQUALITY...

"Karl Sims... I've been given firm orders to chain you to this gurney," stated the FBI agent as she adjusted the wrist restraints and stepped forward. "A liaison from the Intelligence Bureau will be here within the hour to cross-examine you and hopefully arrest you."

As the agent made an attempt to secure my left wrist, I swiftly extracted her .380 from its tacky hip holster. Before it even dawned on her that I was in possession of her firearm, I had the muzzle of the .380 pressed up against her left armpit.

"Who the fuck are you calling a queer?" I sardonically asked after giving the cunt a direct order to raise her hands up over her head.

"Lower that weapon, Karl. I'm a US marshal," stated the now weaponless agent.

"Don't do anything stupid, Carla," shouted the surgeon. "Brandishing a firearm at a US marshal is a federal offense."

"Fuck you and this poorly trained field agent. It's a federal offense and a violation of a moral and social code to sashay into a trauma infirmary and call a critically injured gay man a queer."

"I sincerely apologize for calling you a queer," stated the agent as the phone on her hip began pulsating.

"Don't answer that," I sternly stated while adjusting the safety switch on the .380. "Five of my precious pals were assassinated earlier today and you have the gumption and the impudence to strut in here and insult me while I'm mournfully attempting to make sense of this odious ordeal? I oughta put eight dime-size holes in your diaphragm, you inconsiderate, childish cunt... Now hand me that phone, and when you're done, hike up that tacky-ass skirt and have a seat on this sterilized linoleum floor."

Immediately after being given the touchscreen phone, I called Albert. Albert was one of my openly gay bodyguards. Seconds before he answered, I'd decided that it would be in my best interests to assign Albert the remedial chore of reprimanding this federal deputy and transporting me to a same-sex sanitarium.

Albert answered his phone on the fourth ring. As he said "hello," I could hear the horrendous high-pitched shrieking of several canines in the background...

CHAPTER ELEVEN— SAME-SEX WOOING

Exactly forty-eight seconds after Jessica covertly gave her malicious mastiffs the green light to dispatch the deputized German shepherds, she noticed that the phone affixed to the Defender's right hip was flashing and pulsating.

"Your phone's ringing," shouted Jessica as her mastiffs carried out their assignment.

After glaring at the screen of his cellular phone, Albert accepted the incoming call.

"Hello," stated Albert while diverting his gaze back in the direction of the dogfight.

"It's me, Carla. Where are you?"

"I'm in front of our headquarters, clutching a recoilless rifle."

"It sounds like you're in a dogfighting coliseum," stated Carla, just as one of the German shepherds took its last breath.

"Are you okay?"

"No, I'm not okay. I'm at Michael Reese Hospital. I've been shot in the crotch, Walter's dead, Sharon's dead, my butler was killed, Kevin and Devin are both dead, and now there's this federal agent wearing knockoff Louboutin pumps trying to take me into custody."

"How can I be of service, Commander?" asked Albert as the surgeon eased toward the ER door.

"I need you to come and get me, and transport me to some Same-Sex soil."

"I'm on my way," shouted Albert as I heard the distinct sound of gunfire.

"Were those gunshots?" I asked.

"Yep... A pudgy patrol cop just shot two dogs that belong to one of our lesbian sisters..."

"What the fuck is going on at our command center?"

"Well, babe, the moment the Defenders of Same-Sex Courtship and the gay community heard about you being shot and the others being murdered, the Same-Sex Cabinet sounded the alarm, and now there's approximately twenty-six hundred openly gay armed affiliates outside The Pink House and another eighteen hundred or so LGBT members inside the command center. We're preparing for war, Commander. There are a few hundred cops trying to sway us not to declare war... Your cabinet are confident that we'll wage war later this evening..."

"Come and get me, Albert. I'm serious."

"What floor are you on? And what's your room number?" asked Albert.

"What floor are we on?" I sternly asked while glaring at the surgeon.

"We're on the eighth floor, room 3C."

"Eighth floor, room 3C," I shouted excitedly.

"I'm en route," shouted Albert. "I'll be there in twenty minutes."

"I love you, Albert," I sincerely stated before terminating the call.

"I love you back," shouted Albert.

After suspending the call, I vengefully aimed the .380 at the timorous surgeon.

"Am I in a stable enough condition to abscond this dispensary?" I asked curiously.

"To be honest with you, Karl... I mean Carla... your condition is stable... yet technically critical... It would be irrational and irresponsible of you to check yourself out of this surgery center. For Christ's sake Carla, you were shot in the male organ of copulation and urination. The projectile that perforated your penis was a .270 Winchester. Such projectiles were specifically designed and manufactured to neutralize grizzly bears and polar bears... Not to mention you were shot eight and a half hours ago. I find it odd that you're not at the county morgue freezer being issued a tarnished toe tag, an iodine sponge bath and a death certificate. .270 Winchester rounds have been known to stop an elephant dead in its tracks. You've been out of surgery for fifty six-minutes. If you leave this medical center, you're guaranteed to perish within twenty-four hours."

"I've been raised by Same-Sex Spartans," I nonchalantly stated while aiming the .380 back at the FBI agent. "I've got the resolve of a domesticated dragon. My resilience reminds me of a wounded warrior walking again after being told that he never would. I'm thoroughly convinced that if I check out of this hospital I will not perish... I'm an openly gay man. The odds are always in my favor. The gods are morally obligated to perpetually show me favor. If I stay in this hospital, I'll most likely be killed. And now you're telling me that, if I leave this place, I'll perish within twenty-four hours? FYI arthroscopic surgeon, one of my gallant, lighthearted generals will arrive at this location in the next fifteen or twenty minutes, and I assure you and this absentminded agent that I will be escorted out of this infirmary and ushered to the ER station that's in the cellar of my command center. If I so happen to perish inside The Pink House, then I'll be considered a Same-Sex martyr that died in the name of same-sex marriage. I'd rather die on sovereign Same-Sex soil than be taken into custody by an unattractive agent dressed to the nines in outdated Stella McCartney threads..."

Abdul Robinson

CHAPTER TWELVE— SAME-SEX LOVEMAKING

"Was that Carla?" asked Jessica as Albert put his phone back into its protective case.

"Yes," whispered Albert. "She needs my help... She's at Michael Reese Hospital, eighth floor, room 3C. She mentioned that she's not safe or comfortable at that location and that a federal agent just attempted to take her into custody... I'm en route to her location. You're welcome to participate in this rescue mission but be advised that we may have to shoot our way in and shoot our way out."

"I'd love to participate in the retrieval of our conservative colonel," shouted Jessica as a narc dragged her now-deceased mastiffs out of the busy intersection. "Those cowardly cops killed my dogs," stated Jessica as Albert marched towards his Mercedes-Benz E63 wagon.

"Get in," shouted Albert as he slithered into the driver's seat. Once inside the E63, Albert placed his recoilless rifle on the rear seat. "Buckle up," stated Albert just as the Benz wagon coughed to life.

As Albert bullied his way through the bumper-to-bumper traffic, Jessica adjusted her seatbelt and assessed the interior of the Mercedes. She found it odd that the face of Ravi Perry was tastefully stitched onto the passenger headrest. Unbeknownst to Jessica, Mr. Ravi Petty is a twenty-eight-year-old openly gay black man. That was recently elected president of the NAACP's newly revived Worchester, Massachusetts's chapter. She also had no clue that Perry was a political science professor at Clark University.

"By the way, my name is Albert," stated Albert while make an illegal U-turn on Lake Street.

"Well, it's nice to meet you, Albert. My name is Jessica. I'm a bisexual supermodel that's clearly jaded and somewhat promiscuous..."

"You don't seem the least bit angry that your two dogs were shot and killed just minutes ago by a captious cop," stated Albert as he blew through the first red light they encountered.

"I'm livid that my darlings were just slayed. I'm a very stoic and reserved woman... Therefore, I seldom display or telegraph my emotions. Those two dogs died in the line of duty... Their deaths weren't in vain, and besides, since I was an adolescent I always had the desire to sic my dogs on a deputized K-9."

"Our commander-in-chief will be pleased to hear that your two bullmastiffs attacked a K-9 unit on Same-Sex soil."

Seventeen minutes later, Albert was parking the Benz wagon twelve hundred centimeters from the hospital's front entrance.

"Are you armed?" asked Albert as the two climbed out of the E63.

"Of course I'm armed," whispered Jessica. "I've got a seventeen-shot Taurus in my tote bag, along with a pair of brass knuckles and a full box of nine millimeter shells."

"Roger that," mumbled Albert as they strolled toward the entrance.

"I must say, you do look quite smashing and utterly harmless in those pink fatigues and plastic chukka boots," stated Jessica just as they entered the hospital.

"Well, you look like a spoiled, entitled debutante in those designer duds and overpriced Bally boots," shouted Albert after winking at the armed security guard.

"I saw the way you gazed at that security guard," whispered Jessica as the two came to a halt in front of the elevator.

"Mind your business, young lady."

"Do you have a boyfriend?" asked Jessica.

"Yes... I've got a boyfriend. Quite a few, actually," stated Albert as they walked into the elevator enclosure.

"Do you have a boyfriend?" asked Albert after pressing the button for the eighth floor.

"Of course I have a boyfriend. Quiet as kept, my boyfriend has a boyfriend, and just so you know, I've got a girlfriend that I fleeced from my ex-girlfriend."

"Be sure not to tell our commander about your boyfriend having a boyfriend, and sure as hell don't convey to her that you're romantically involved with a dame that you poached from a former lover of yours."

Albert and Jessica exited the elevator on the eighth floor. Neither was surprised to see three armed security guards seated behind a sentry desk. Albert nodded at the three guards stationed at the watchman's desk before marching over to greet the Saudi Arabian female receptionist.

As Albert approached the receptionist's counter, Jessica batted her eyelashes and coquettishly waved at the three security guards. As the three guards appraised Jessica's heart-shaped derriere and lustrous Shirley Temple curls, Albert covertly extracted a wad of fifty-dollar bills from his left rear pocket. After politely informing the receptionist that he was interested in visiting his younger brother Karl Sims, he cunningly slid the bundle of bills over the counter.

After looking over her right shoulder, the Saudi Arabian receptionist quickly and surreptitiously seized the little heap of fifty-dollar bills. Just as Jessica was exchanging contact information with one of the handsome security guards, the receptionist was instructing Albert that Mr. Sims was in room 3C.

"Good job distracting those dudes," whispered Albert as they made their way down the ER corridor.

It took Albert and Jessica a little under thirteen seconds to reach room 3C.

"Greetings, Commander," shouted Albert the moment he crossed the threshold.

"Who's the damsel?" asked Carla the second Jessica entered the room.

"Her name is Jessica," stated Albert after giving Carla a curt kiss on the forehead. "She's an LGBT affiliate babe. She's solid and seductive."

"Do you know one another?" asked Carla after she noticed Jessica and the FBI agent gaping at each other.

"Yes, Carla. We've met before," stated Jessica while sashaying over to the young lady seated on the floor with her dress hiked up over her waist. "And I assure you she's not here on behalf of the Federal Bureau. She's a functioning junkie from New Jersey. Her name is Veronica. She's a pill-popping, pussy-popping gypster."

"If I'm a pussy-popping gypster, you're a coke-and-molly-peddling grifter," shouted Veronica while glaring at Jessica. "And I assure you Carla, she's no LGBT affiliate. She's never even tasted fresh pussy."

"You shut your mouth, cunt," stated Jessica while standing over Veronica.

"So you're not a federal agent?" asked Carla while aiming the .380 at Veronica's torso.

"Yes, I'm a federal agent... But technically my superiors didn't authorize this vulpine visit. I apologize Carla, I had no idea you were a woman of power, substance and taste. Please don't kill me."

"Who sent you?" Carla calmly asked while gazing over at the scared surgeon.

"A dainty, diabolical damsel by the name of Catilina paid me eight grand and two kilos of Afghani black tar to simply stroll in here, read you your rights, secure your ankles with leg irons and handcuff you to that gurney."

"I oughta have my pal Albert here remove your entrails and ration them out to the alley rats that are plaguing the south side of Chicago," stated Carla while retracting the hammer on the .380.

"Where's Catilina?" asked Albert after spitting a mouthful of stringy, thick phlegm into Veronica's pie-shaped face.

"She's parading around South Beach in a liver-colored Ferrari that's topless and opulent," shouted Veronica as tears coated her corneas. "Her contact info is logged in my phone under the moniker Cat-Eyes – she's number 6 on the speed-dial. I was given an austere directive to contact her the second I completed the dreadful task of shackling you and silencing the self-absorbed surgeon."

"Excuse me, Carla," whispered Jessica, "but can I please be awarded the monumental chore of dismembering this jealous Jezebel?"

"She's a thoughtless Judas," shouted Albert as Jessica extracted the seventeen-shot Taurus from her designer tote bag.

"I'm sorry, Carla," shouted Veronica as urine abruptly began squirting from her vagina. "I can help you all outwit, entrap and allocate mortification to the callous Catilina and her Canadian cohorts."

CHAPTER THIRTEEN— SAME-SEX MARRIAGE

As several drag queens hauled the cop into the auditorium, I noticed that Loyd's disposition abruptly changed.

"Pardon the intrusion, Sebastian," shouted one of the drag queens, "but this inebriated narc has no adoration for same-sex courting. He was found on the grounds slurring anti-gay jokes. This prick was also observed taunting the transsexual teens that are outside chanting EQUALITY jargon."

"OFF with his head," shouted a transgendered swordsman wielding two bronze Oriental swords.

"As you can see, Sebastian, we wasted no time placing this despicable detective under arrest."

"Let's hang the son of a bitch from the nearest light pole," shouted the swordsman clutching the two scimitars.

"Be advised, Sebastian, that the pencil-dick perp is clearly under the influence of alcohol and cocaine," shouted a drag queen that was in possession of Detective Stevenson's police-issued firearm. "His pupils are dilated, his breath smells of vodka and anchovies, there's a white powdery substance surrounding his left and right nostrils; he's alert and thoroughly aware that he's on Same-Sex soil. To subjugate this creep was a simple task. It took me and a few queens twenty-six seconds or so to subdue this jerk."

"Good job, ladies," I gleefully stated after giving the queens instructions to usher the narcissistic narc to the podium and chain him to Carla's granite throne.

As the queens dragged the cop onto the platform, I was utterly surprised to see Loyd step forward and send a flying knee into the cop's abdomen. The knee he devilishly delivered to the cop's midsection caused the detective to vomit uncontrollably. The matter discharged from his stomach smelled like the virulent juices found in the inner confines of a city dumpster. The cotton panties that were shoved into his mouth earlier were now cloaked in noxious puke.

"Kill him," shouted a bisexual butcher brandishing a box-cutter.

"Let's force-feed him live leeches," shouted a lesbian, loading a musket. The thought of force-feeding this cop live bloodsucking worms like my comrade suggested seemed and sounded grand.

"Do you know this guy?" I asked Loyd as the Same-Sex Operatives cheered and raved at the sight of the cop barfing.

"Yes," shouted Loyd. "This closed-minded weasel is my coworker and partner from the homicide squad. I have wanted to knee him in the stomach for several months now. He's a racist, homophobic hater. During our partnership, he's conveyed to me that he has an irrational hatred for homosexuals and homosexuality. Although he's not directly linked to the iniquity that befell my queen and her best friends, I've got audio footage of this prejudiced coward voicing his irrational hostility towards Carla and members of the gay community."

"What's going on, Loyd?" asked Stevenson while glaring at the drag queen that was designated to chain him to Carla's throne.

"Tell the junkie what's going on, Loyd," shouted a gay gangster clutching an alloy machete.

"It doesn't take a physicist to figure out that I'm Carla's fiancé, and you've been taken into custody by glamorous dames that have zero tolerance for biased heterosexuals that luxuriate in teasing the transgendered and taunting the transsexual."

"I need medical attention," screamed Stevenson. "I'm certain that my pelvis is fractured in multiple places. That flamboyant fellow in the floral-printed girdle whacked me in my pelvis with a fucking jackhammer."

"I sure did, and I'll do it again if you muster up the courage to say anything cruel about same-sex parents or same-sex marriage," stated the queen, twirling the twenty-pound sledgehammer as if it was a slender baton.

"It doesn't surprise me that you're one of them," stated Stevenson after spitting sputum onto the throne that sat to the left of the throne he was chained to. "I often sensed that you had some sugar in your tank."

"I'm in no mood to hear you two verbally spar," I stated frankly after retrieving the cotton panties from the large puddle of puke.

Abruptly, after retrieving the puke-covered panties, I swaggered over to Detective Stevenson and crammed the sullied knickers back into the detective's mouth. Carla's cabinet and my associates clapped and squealed in delight after I dexterously wedged the panties into the cop's mouth.

"FYI, Same-Sex Sentinels, we will deal with this lad according to his merit," I sternly stated while cleaning the puke from between my fingers.

"Settle down everyone... so Carla's fiancé can continue giving us a candid digest on the calculative culprit that's responsible for murdering our cofounders and egregiously wounding our commander-in-chief."

As Loyd cleared his throat and stepped up to the microphone, I marveled at the slew of openly gay Defenders that filled the auditorium. The plethora of weaponry gave credence to the notion that the Defenders of Same-Sex Courtship were not only prepared for war, but were theoretically in a favorable position to vindictively declare war on the gay bashers of the United States. After Loyd approached the microphone, a respectful silence fell over the auditorium.

"Be advised that Carla is in critical yet stable condition. After undergoing several hours of testis surgery, the doctors and on-call surgeons ensured me that our commander will be okay. The surgery was conducted gracefully and tastefully. Although I spent approximately six and a half hours at Carla's bedside, I was unable to extract any intel from her. Due to the morphine, anesthesia and tubes down her throat, she was unable to communicate with me. I kissed her a little over eighty-three times before leaving the ER unit...

"As I said earlier, the three brown Ferraris were last seen headed east on I-57. In my satchel I have six thousand stills of Catilina Ortega. Many of the photographs are pics that I personally fleeced from her Facebook page and Instagram profile. This bitch has a tally of twenty-two thousand followers, several offshore accounts, no Twitter account, an old MySpace profile, and no Wikipedia page. She also has several fraudulent profiles on eight dating websites.

"She's a regimented cunt that has an IQ and the disposition of a mobster-like mercenary. She's connected and respected by cartel bosses. She's made a name for herself in the underworld and the black market. In her former life, she did some extensive modeling. She's an ex-exotic dancer that still dabbles in the escort service genre.

"Somehow she's managed to obtain a license to carry a firearm. Her weapon of choice is the AK-47. She's Slovakian, yet speaks with a German accent. She's also fluent in six indigenous dialects. I was unable to obtain intel on the true color of her eyes and hair. The bitch is a diplomatic chameleon that's intimately familiar with the covert arts and espionage. Although she's had no military training, she's a modern-day minuteman. Rumor has it that she once defaced a Liberace sculpture and torched several LGBT floats that were scheduled to be showcased in the 2014 gay pride parade. And to top it all off, my sources deep within Homeland Security have shabby evidence that semi-links Catilina to several homicides that involved aspiring same-sex parents that were affluent, influential and politically connected."

"She sounds like a witch that's well-read and well-bred," shouted a Liechtensteiner lesbian carrying a sharp sickle.

"She's a witch indeed," stated Loyd. "As far as being well-bred and well-read, that's yet to be established. Her FBI file divulged that she's a tyrant that's under no one's tutelage. In regards to one of the homicides she's allegedly involved in, the virtuous victims were a loving same-sex couple, newlyweds from Arizona. The two Caucasian males both had the aspiration of someday being awarded the right to adopt several pre-pubescent orphans from Uganda. Both martyrs were decapitated, although the skulls of both men were never recovered. Their scrotums were discovered in a plush perambulator that was parked in their neighbor's nursery."

"Does this cunt have a personal vendetta against the gay colonies that now pepper the United States?" asked the MMA cage fighter, brandishing a poisonous dart.

"She's not gay, however she has had a few sexual liaisons with a client of hers when she was affiliated with the sex trafficking industry. There's no evidence to suggest that she has a vindictive axe to grind against same-sex entities, yet she's made it clear to law enforcement agencies, biased politicians and gay advocates that she and her two accomplished accomplices are enthusiastically prepared to eradicate any member of the LBGT society, for capital and political favors."

"Why were our commander and her loyal lieutenants targeted?" asked a young man in pink leggings, inserting .223 rounds into a hundred-round drum magazine that he detached from his assault rifle...

CHAPTER FOURTEEN— SAME-SEX NEWLYWEDS

While seated in her rust-colored Ferrari outside Michael Reese Hospital, Catilina impatiently waited for Agent Stephanie Brooks to contact her via text message.

Sixteen minutes had passed and the infamous Catilina had become antsy. Earlier the same day she paid Stephanie eight grand and seventy-two ounces of heroin to storm into Carla's ER suite and place a pair of restraints around her ankles and a set of manacles around her wrists. Unbeknownst to Agent Brooks, the one hundred sixty fifty-dollar bills that Catilina had given her were low-quality counterfeit greenbacks, and the two kilos of Afghani black tar heroin she was given was actually chocolate cake mix combined with athlete's foot powder.

While eagerly waiting for her iPhone 6 to pulsate and chirp, Catilina skillfully screwed the pint-sized suppressor onto the muzzle of her twenty-one-shot German Luger. After attaching the suppressor to the Ruger, Catilina placed the weapon into her leather-trimmed Kiton tote bag and swiftly slithered out of the convertible.

As she made her way to the entrance of the hospital, several female nurses and two male orderlies gawked at Catilina. While the two Indian orderlies gazed at Catilina's jiggling derriere, the self-conscious nurses gaped, glared and assessed Catilina's overall appearance. The female LPNs and RNs found it peculiar that her Christian Dior sundress was silk, sheer and strapless. Her lime-colored garter belt and lemon-colored brassiere could be seen through the delicate fabric. The

Lugano tennis bracelet that encircled her left wrist out-glistened the Jack Kelége engagement ring that dangled from the Martin Katz choker clasped around her neck.

The pricey wig she had on cloaked her own radiant mane. The wig in question was the exact wig that she had snatched off of Carla's crown nine hours before, during the malignant massacre she personally facilitated. Perched atop the wig now sat a diamond-studded tiara. The tiara was also adorned with diamond-encrusted butterflies. The headband was a trinket that Catilina fleeced from a Jewish jeweler at the Monaco rare jewels exhibition. The tiara alone was Catilina's sly way of flaunting a touch of nobility.

After smiling at the orderlies and rolling her eyes at the RNs and LPNs, she entered the hospital.

"Hi, handsome," shouted Catilina as she sashayed past the armed security guard standing near the front entrance.

Before the security guard could suck in his gut, poke out his chest and reward her "Hi, handsome" greeting with a witty womanizing remark, she had already made a beeline to the elevator shaft. After pushing the circular button to summon the elevator, Catilina smiled and waved at the registered nurses and floor nurses that peeped and peered at her from behind medical clipboards and frameless eyeglasses.

"That's a badass tote bag," shouted a young lady dressed in scrubs and a surgeon's smock.

"Thanks. It's a Kitons," whispered Catilina just as the elevator doors opened.

The freight elevator was empty, just as she had hoped. After winking at the dame in the surgeon's smock, Catilina stepped inside the elevator, hoping that the tote bag admirer wouldn't set foot in the elevator. As the young lady did an about-face and sauntered toward a crying toddler, Catilina pressed button number 8 on the digitized wall panel.

Abruptly after the elevator doors closed, Catilina extracted the twenty-one-shot German Ruger from the Kiton tote bag. As the elevator soared upward to the eighth floor, her nipples hardened and her heart rate accelerated. Within seconds, the elevator reached the eighth floor. As the doors opened, she spotted two dashing dispensary deputies standing to the left of a vintage vending machine. Catilina stepped out of the elevator and immediately opened fire on the hospital cops. The overweight receptionist heard the barrage of muffled gunshots, yet her eyes remained glued to the thirteen-inch touchscreen iPad that rested on her lap.

The two hospital guards were both struck in the face and chest, and both synchronously fell to the floor. Just as the burly receptionist sensed Catilina's presence, she smelled the odor of what she believed to be matchsticks burning.

"Something's burning, guys," she shouted while raising her head.

The instant she raised her head, Catilina squeezed the trigger and two 9 mm projectiles entered the skull, ruptured the cerebellum and simultaneously silenced the receptionist. The roly-poly receptionist died with her mouth and eyes wide open. The iPad on her lap hit the floor as she lifelessly slid out of the swivel chair.

As Catilina incautiously made her way down the hall, she could smell Agent Brooks' cheap unisex perfume. Catilina reached room 3C in less than ten seconds.

Four seconds later, she stormed into the room with the callousness and malice of a heat-seeking missile. The sinful Catilina was able to let off seven rounds before Carla took aim and sent six .380 shells into Catilina's curvaceous frame.

Two of the seven rounds that were fired from Catilina's weapon struck Albert in the torso and abdomen. The bullets sent him crashing into a fully functional incubator. Two more of the seven rounds hit Stephanie in the right ear and left elbow. The fifth round fired from Catilina's Ruger ricocheted off an oxygen tank and struck Carla in the left foot. The last two projectiles that Catilina intentionally fired in Jessica's direction pierced her right jaw, shattering her cheekbone.

Just as the seventh bullet entered Jessica's right shoulder and cracked her rotator cuff, the startled Carla aimed the .380 at Catilina and pulled the trigger six times. All six projectiles struck Catilina in one-second intervals. The first two rounds struck her liver. The third round discharged from the .380 struck Catilina in the heart, leaving a penny-sized hole in her aorta. The shot to the heart is what primarily neutralized Catilina, yet it wasn't the round that killed her. Precisely one second after the bullet pierced her aorta; another .380 shell hit her in the base of her tongue. After severing her tongue from its base, the bullet lodged in the underside of her tongue. Immediately after being hit in the jaw, Catilina dropped her twenty-one-shot German Luger and lunged into a medicinal pushcart. The round responsible for affecting Catilina's death was the sixth round discharged from the .380. That bullet struck her in the gallbladder.

"Are you okay, Albert?" asked Carla as Catilina justly perished.

"I can't breathe," stated Albert while blood gushed out of the hole in his abdomen.

"Don't you die on me," shouted Carla as she dialed Loyd's phone number.

Just as Loyd answered his phone, the terrified surgeon began crawling out from behind a breathing apparatus with the look of a frightened kitten.

CHAPTER FIFTEEN— SAME-SEX NUPTIALS

"Our allies at the Pentagon and the Terrorist Division are convinced that Carla was targeted for her flamboyant belief in EQUALITY and same-sex nuptials," stated Loyd as the phone in his left back pocket chirped. "Pardon me, comrades, I've got an incoming call. I'm sure it's Carla since she's the only breathing entity that has my cellphone number."

The League of EQUALITY INSURGENTS suspended their yammering as Loyd answered his phone.

"Hi, cupcake," stated Loyd after putting Carla on speakerphone.

"Where the fuck are you?" asked Carla as Loyd held the phone up to the wireless microphone.

"I'm at The Pink House, briefing your cabinet and LGBT family on the status of your condition."

"During your two-hour absence, a wretched witch stormed into my hospital room and opened fire. Albert's sprawled out on the floor coughing up blood... I'm sure he was hit in the nape of his neck. An FBI agent is on the floor in front of my bed. She was hit multiple times. I'm certain she died forty seconds ago. I was struck in the foot and Albert's lady friend was hit in the shoulder."

"Are you serious, babe?" asked Loyd as dozens of members began weeping and cursing.

"Yes, I'm serious. The surgeon is going to get help now. And what the hell are you doing at The Pink House?"

"I came here to brief your cabinet and comrades on your condition and to officially pounce out of the closet."

"Get your ass here," shouted Carla. "And don't you dare leave my side again. Someone wants me dead."

"I'm on my way, babe," shouted Loyd as Sebastian grabbed the phone out of his hand.

"Are you okay, Commander?"

"Who the fuck is this?" asked Carla.

"It's me, Sebastian. Be advised that it's pretty intense here at headquarters. Thousands of openly gay operatives from the gay community are here in the auditorium, cradling their weapons of choice, waiting on your message strategist to confirm that you support our decision to declare war against homophobic heterosexuals that are bitchy, biased and blasphemous... The news of you being wounded and the others being killed has the gay community on edge. Hundreds of us are enraged and lusting to wreak havoc on those that oppose Same-Sex Courtship. My question to you, Commander, is can you please do the honors of awarding us the right to bear arms against every taxpayer that's in cahoots with the pompous politicians that have a sincere desire to veto the Same-Sex Marriage Bill?"

"Although it's utterly evident that we have probable cause to lynch biased legislators, we're not at liberty to respond in a manner that constitutes radicalism and terrorism. Certain parties will indeed be held accountable for the travesty and traumatic tragedy that unfolded at my estate. Good job rallying the transgendered and transsexual troops. I declare and decree that our bisexual battalion and lesbian lunatics stand down, yet stand their ground until further notice. Are we clear, Sebastian?"

"As clear as crystal," stated Sebastian while dramatically rolling his eyes as if he was an annoyed damsel.

"Now put my fiancé back on the phone," shouted Carla as several first responders frantically entered her hospital room.

"Your man left two minutes ago. I'm sure he's en route to your location... Inform my cabinet that The Pink House is to be protected by all available means, and that I'll contact them in several hours with the details of our next move. Extend my love and adoration to all my LGBT comrades. I hate to terminate this call but the EMTs and several investigators are urging me to hang up the phone."

"Be strong, Carla," shouted a Japanese lesbian wielding a small revolver.

"She'll be okay," stated Sebastian after Carla terminated the call.

"How can you be certain that she'll be alright?" asked a bisexual brute brandishing a bayonet.

"Because weaker homosexuals have survived harder times than this."

"So what do we do now?" asked a fellow sitting on the lap of his boyfriend.

"We march in the streets, and chant equality ballads and same-sex courtship carols," shouted Sebastian. "And the first person that says something inappropriate about our sexual preference will be woefully tackled and beaten with the stocks of our rifles."

"Sebastian, there's a negotiator from Quantico on line one," shouted a member of Carla's cabinet. "She requested to converse with the earl or viscount of this Same-Sex Infantry."

"You tell that negligent negotiator that the marquis of this Same-Sex Dynasty does not and will not negotiate with heterosexual Pharisees."

"I informed the negotiator that the Defenders of Same-Sex Courtship has an extensive history of NOT NEGOTIATING with self-righteous heterosexuals. The negotiator insisted that he speak with our president before blood is spilled on our soil."

"Let the record reflect that his emphatic demand to speak to our captain has merit. Our vengeful, vehement Defenders are outside;

brandishing hand grenades and aiming assorted weapons at the cops. The cops have taken two-dozen or so of our members into custody. Shots have been fired. One of our comrades sicced her bullmastiffs on a deputized K-9, homosexuals from all walks of life are outside, many are toting rifles and revolvers, some are wielding swords, battle axes and flamethrowers, and as you know, the knighted guardians of The Pink House are outside clutching rocket launchers, machine guns, and crossbows. It's monumentally intense out there.

"At the moment, we outnumber the cops sixteen to one, but our sources at the Police Department assured us that the National Guard and SEAL Team 8 are en route to facilitate order and neutralize all homosexual hostiles.

"I'm guessing there's approximately a hundred or so cops outside trying to restore order, and there's at least twenty-nine hundred LGBT affiliates. Out of the twenty-nine hundred, I'd say at least twenty-three hundred of us are armed and fabulous. And that twenty-nine hundred doesn't include the two thousand or so Defenders that are in this auditorium, and the several hundred armed transsexuals that are guarding the foyer."

"It's paramount that you converse with the negotiator before a war and riot ensues, because when the National Guard and other military personnel arrive on scene, our militia will be viewed and categorized as spleenful, inimical terrorists that must be viciously vanquished at all costs."

"Are you suggesting that we rationally retreat like spineless sex addicts?" asked a fellow wearing a pink evening gown and clutching an arbalest.

"I'm suggesting that if we're going to wage war, then it'll be sagacious and sly of us to strike now before their cavalry shows up in full body armor. The leaders of the armed forces aren't going to let us stand in the streets wielding weapons. It's the twenty-first century – our behavior won't be tolerated. The government will covertly sanction and launch an assortment of drone attacks."

"And we'll die as foolish, brave martyrs that didn't familiarize themselves or their same-sex coalition with the rules of engagement when it came to warfare and diplomacy."

"Is the negotiator still on line one?" asked Sebastian after retrieving his rocket launcher.

"Yes, she's still on the line," shouted the cabinet member.

"Good... Inform the wench that we have Detective Stevenson in our custody, and if the National Guard come within a three block radius of our Alcazar fortress, I'll personally carve the word EQUALITY across Stevenson's forehead and torso using a jackknife that once belonged to Boy George..."

CHAPTER SIXTEEN— SAME-SEX ADOPTION

"Excuse me, Mr. President... I hate to sour your evening with this news, but we have a situation in Illinois that's extremely foreign, flagrant and fragile."

"I'm in no mood to hear about the gang violence that's scourging Illinois," shouted the president after snorting a two-inch line of granulated prescription pain pills that belonged to the first lady.

"The situation that warrants your attention is twice as grim and twice as grave as Chicago's gun/gang violence."

"What's the situation?" asked the president as he fiddled with the rolled-up two-dollar bill that he used repeatedly on a daily basis to transport granulated pills up his flared nostril.

"Ten hours ago, Sir, six openly gay civilians of the LGBT community were egregiously gunned down. Four of the victims perished on the scene. One of the victims that miraculously survived the ominous onslaught was a transgendered chap by the name of Karl Sims. The moniker Karl currently goes by is CARLA; net worth, three hundred million. He's an industrialist that was shot in the penis after three masked intruders strolled into his homestead. During the home invasion, five of his cronies were critically injured. The first responders had Karl airlifted to Michael Reese Hospital. Four of his gay pals were transported to the Cook County morgue. The other survivor was transported to a local hospital. FYI Mr. President, Karl AKA Carla is the commander-in-chief of a homosexual hit squad that's charitable, clannish and callous. They're known in West Hollywood and all throughout America as the Defenders of Same-Sex Courtship. Our competent sources at Langley conveyed to me that this same-sex brigade has a little over five thousand members. And eighty-five percent of their members are trained insurgents, iniquitous in their treatment, that find solace in torturing captious heterosexuals that oppose same-sex lovemaking.

"Hours after Carla and her companions were ambushed and injured, the calamitous tidings reached the gay community and now there's several thousand armed homosexuals on the streets of Illinois, dressed in combat gear and designer duds. Homeland Security received a call from the mayor and the commissioner requesting immediate military assistance, because hundreds of the gay protestors are in possession of hand grenades and other explosives.

"We've got eyes on the ground and they've confirmed that there's at least eighteen hundred demonstrators standing outside of their headquarters, brandishing picket signs and weapons of every make and model. I've got live video and audio footage of these openly gay men and women toting assault rifles and wielding bazookas."

"You're full of shit," shouted the president after snorting another long thin line of finely crushed pain pills. "Members of the gay community are pansies, pushovers and punks... Surely you don't expect me to believe that there's a small army of homosexuals standing outside of a skyscraper brandishing firearms, swords and rocket launchers as if they're ready to declare war?"

"Mr. President, I swear to you, this intelligence that I'm divulging to you is serious and truthful. The slaying of four of their comrades and the assassination attempt on their chief has the LGBT community in a unanimous uproar. Openly gay civilians from all walks of life are making their way to The Pink House."

"What's The Pink House?" asked President Dotson.

"The Pink House is a gargantuan convention center that's been refurbished and converted into a majestic command center for Carla and the Defenders of Same-Sex Courtship. We've yet to plant a set of eyes inside The Pink House, but a confidential informant that's been superbly reliable in the past informed the Gang Task Force Unit that there's about twenty-six hundred armed gay soldiers inside The Pink

House, including Carla's clever cabinet."

"You speak of these harmless queers as if they're malignant marines that possess the perspective of merciless mercenaries," shouted the president after snorting the remainder of the pain pills.

"I assure you, Mr. President, that these aren't run-of-the-mill homosexuals. They're from a lineage that's selfless and Spartan-like. It's as if they're under John Gotti's tutelage. The urban legends that stem from this platoon of misfits would frighten Jack the Ripper. Homeland Security has ordered the National Guard to facilitate the neutralization and hopefully the eradication of these fags... Our allies in Congress and Beverly Hills are hoping that you will declare the Defenders of Same-Sex Courtship enemies of the state and set in motion a Special Ops drone attack that'll flatten their clubhouse and exterminate these equality avengers once and for all."

"That's GENOCIDE, dipshit," shouted President Dotson. "I wouldn't dare even entertain the thought of launching a drone attack on a legion of lesbians and openly gay US citizens. I should have you and the gutless, gluttonous gamblers in Congress stoned for requesting that I devilishly nullify a colony of affectionate gay people that are mourning the death of four of their tribal members."

"Mr. President, be advised that a negotiator, along with a terrorism analyst, have been ordered to open up a dialogue with the primary Defender of their squadron. The provincial admiral of the Same-Sex Regime declined to converse with the negotiator. However, one of their lesbian liaisons did inform the terrorism analyst that they have a Detective Stevenson – badge number 061784 – in their custody and that if the National Guard comes within a three block radius of their fortress, one of their cohorts will carve the phrase EQUALITY across Stevenson's forehead and lower back."

"The Cook County sheriff's certain that Detective Stevenson is being held against his will by these gay musketeers?" asked President Dotson while suppressing the unprofessional snicker that seeped out of his mouth.

"This is a somber matter that's controversial and on the verge of spawning into America's worst nightmare..."

"Calm down," shouted Dotson. "Relax and pour yourself a cocktail. There's some vodka in the bottle rack that's been imported from Sri

Lanka. You're always so intense. If the gays in Illinois are protesting, picketing, boycotting and doing some minor looting, then I'm sure that the police force in Illinois can handle a platoon of punks."

"For Christ's sake, Mr. President, this is a state of emergency. I ask that you view the live video footage of these pissed off homosexuals."

Six minutes later, President Dotson was reviewing footage of the Defenders of Same-Sex Courtship.

"Who the fuck are these people?" asked Dotson while gazing at the jumbo plasma screen and spotting eight drag queens in pink fatigues, clutching German rocket launchers.

"They're LGBT affiliates, Sir."

"There's hundreds of them," shouted the president as he spotted a mob of same-sex parents clutching hand grenades and homemade Molotov cocktails.

"FYI, Sir, the commissioner tallied the number of armed queers and he's certain there's a few thousand armed civilians on the outer perimeter of the property, and several thousand armed individuals inside the building. We have intel that shots have been fired. So far, eighty-six armed protestors have been arrested. There've been approximately two casualties – one of the LGBT members ordered two bullmastiffs to attack the Lake County K-9 Unit. The mastiffs killed two of their most trusted bomb-sniffing German shepherds. The sheriffs neutralized the mastiffs, and as you can see, those are the two mastiffs sprawled out in the intersection. The two deceased canines were swiftly transported to the Lake County K-9 mortuary."

"Are those machine guns and swords they're wielding?" asked Dotson after diverting his attention to a transgendered vixen pointing an Uzi at a pudgy patrolman. "Have they made any demands?"

"No, Sir. For the most part, they've been taunting law enforcement, chanting equality hymns and brandishing their weapons at officers. Mrs. Jackson, a terrorism analyst at Quantico, believes that if these gay insurgents are not swiftly decimated, queers across the globe will start emulating this taboo behavior. An LGBT advocate had the audacity to tell one of our noble negotiators that the Defenders of Same-Sex Courtship don't negotiate with heterosexuals."

"Who's their leader?" asked President Dotson as he watched thirteen armed bisexuals exit a flesh-colored shuttle bus.

"Their administrator is an openly gay brute whose name is Karl Sims. He's an aspiring diva that goes by the name Carla."

"I vividly recall you stating that this Karl character is at Michael Reese Hospital," stated Dotson as he witnessed a transgendered teen spit in the face of a US marshal dressed in SWAT gear.

"Yes, Mr. President. He's at Michael Reese Hospital undergoing testicle surgery."

"Deploy the National Guard, and tell them they're to stand down unless I authorize them to engage with these same-sex extremists. Contact Homeland Security, the commissioner and the mayor, and convey to them that deploying drones to dispatch a threat that's amorous, lighthearted and salacious is out of the question. Notify the Cook County sheriffs and Lake County sheriffs and advise them not to arrest another picketer. Advise the negotiators and terrorism analysts to continue their quest for attempting to open up a dialogue with the co-captain of this regime of same-sex radicals.

"Instruct my cabinet that the LGBT members will not be treated as formidable combatants until trustworthy evidence is received that their weapons are authentic and loaded. For all we know, they could all be in possession of costume weaponry like that used in blockbuster films."

"We shouldn't have to authenticate their weaponry, Sir. It's obvious that those rifles and rocket launchers are real. What is with you? And this regard you have for homosexuals?"

"I understand them," shouted President Dotson. "I understand the laws of EQUALITY. I understand their frustration from being judged, criticized, and ostracized by biased Americans that don't grasp the concept of INDIVIDUALITY."

"You sound like one of those gay advocates that support same-sex adoption..."

"I sound like a gay advocate, huh?" asked Dotson as he gawked at the armed transsexuals that guarded The Pink House entrance. "What if I told you I once had sexual relations with a jock back in college? Would you judge me?" asked the president. "Would you view me as less than a man, less than your commander-in-chief, less than presidential? What if I told you that I utterly enjoyed the experimental liaison I had with the captain of the lacrosse team? What if I told you that the desire to court, woo, seduce and penetrate another man is inherently present within my spirit? What if I told you that the first lady is attracted to damsels, preferably promiscuous video vixens? What if I told you that the first lady loves the pleasant aroma of fresh pussy and chilled muscatel? What if I told you that the first lady has a girlfriend in Thailand that she's sexually active with? Would you judge and ridicule my wife? Would you deem her unfit, unstable and slutty? How would you respond if I informed you and the secretary of defense that I've had a schoolboy crush on you ever since you complimented my beryl studded cufflinks at last year's inauguration ceremony?"

CHAPTER SEVENTEEN— SAME-SEX PARENTING

Seconds after ending the call with my hubby and Sebastian, I could hear frightened screams and disquieting cries from the EMS personnel and other first responders in the hallway outside of my room. The disturbing cries and frightened screams assured me that Catilina had injured a few LPNs and pediatricians before storming into my room.

"Are you okay, Mr. Sims?" asked a uniformed officer as he raced into my room with his weapon drawn.

"No, I'm not okay. I've been shot in the foot."

"Doctors and EMTs are en route, but I'm going to need you to drop that weapon."

After dropping the .380 on the floor beside the bed, the officer knelt down and secured the weapon that was next to Catilina and the firearm that was next to Albert's lady friend.

"What the hell happened in here?" asked the cop as he knelt next to Catilina and checked her pulse.

I ignored the question and gazed over at Albert. My observation told me that he had expired seconds ago. Before I could make sense of the attack, several paramedics, a few surgeons and a dozen uniformed officers marched into the room. The surgeons and paramedics were clearly befuddled and utterly appalled to be greeted by three corpses and a reinjured transgendered damsel in distress.

I watched in silence as Albert, Catilina and Jessica were placed onto stretchers and ushered to the trauma unit. The surgeon that was now administering medical attention to my foot was a blue-eyed male that reminded me of George Michael. His breath smelled like Juicy Fruit gum and his teeth were peppered with coffee stains. The platinum wedding band that encircled his ring finger telegraphed the fact that he was spoken for and off the market. The LGBT insignia that was engraved across the outer surface of the band was a majestic telltale sign that he was romantically involved with a same-sex knight. The twinkle in his right eye was solid proof that he was happy and sexually satisfied. Yet, the sad fact that he intentionally avoided making eye contact with me swayed me to believe that the surgeon was a closet homosexual.

As the surgeon treated my wound, I overtly hiked up my hospital gown and gave him an unobstructed glimpse of the same-sex marriage emblem and LGBT insignia that I recently had tattooed on my inner left thigh. As the blue-eyed surgeon marveled at the same-sex marriage emblem, I felt myself getting drowsy. My vision began to blur. I felt the gurney I was on being disunited from the iron wall hasp.

"Where am I going?" I mumbled to myself as the morphine and anesthesia began to claim my consciousness.

"Hey... I'm thirsty... Where's Loyd...? What time is it...? I'm hungry... Where's my wig...? Has anyone seen my Prada shades?" I knew I was jabbering and babbling thoughtlessly. The administered sedatives had me feeling sluggish and inebriated.

After two minutes or so of barking ludicrous orders at the MDs, GPs, physicians and orderlies, I felt myself fully succumb to the anesthesia.

...THREE AND A HALF HOURS LATER...

The intoxicating redolence of Loyd's unisex cologne is primarily what greeted me the instant my senses were abruptly restored.

"Hi, chocolate drop," shouted Loyd as my eyes fluttered open.

"Where the fuck have you been?" I tartly asked as he planted several wet kisses on my left cheek.

"I've been here for the last three hours trying to figure out why KARMA and calamity have graced you with their woeful presence. What the fuck is going on, babe? Why do Catilina and her constituents want you dead?"

"How the fuck should I know? I was in our love nest discussing same-sex affairs when that cunt and two of her goblins charged into the den, brandishing hunting rifles. Before we could detect their presence, a succession of shots rang out. I recall hearing Heather scream just before I was struck in the penis. Before blacking out, I observed Devin coughing up blood and crashing into a gun rack. The next thing I knew, I woke up harnessed to a damn stretcher."

"Calm down, my queen," whispered Loyd as a nurse practitioner checked my vitals.

"He's right, Mr. Sims. It's best that you calm down," stated the nurse practitioner. "Your blood pressure and anxiety levels are already dangerously high."

"How can I calm down when trained assassins have been contracted to vanquish me and my caring cronies?"

"Check this out, babe," whispered Loyd as he held my right hand. "Catilina's dead. We've got intel that she was hired to dispatch you and your pals. The motive has yet to be discovered. Funds from a Jessica Henderson's Swiss account were electronically transferred into an offshore account that belonged to Catilina Ortega. Jessica Henderson died two hours ago during a botched surgery. Unbeknownst to you, your friend Albert led Jessica to your location. We have some minor circumstantial evidence that ties Albert to the murder-for-hire plot..."

"Albert wouldn't dare be in cahoots with scum like Catilina," I shouted while gazing into Loyd's cinnamon-colored eyes. "And he sure as hell had nothing to do with me being wounded and my pals being slayed. Albert's a tried-and-true loyalist. He's a true blue, steadfast knight that I personally knighted. And if you insist on brazenly stating that he's somehow connected to the monsters that killed my loyal friends, I'm afraid I'm going to ask you to leave and find another queen to court."

"I apologize, babe," stated Loyd after planting a thoughtful kiss on the tip of my nose. "You're right. There's no way in hell Albert would forsake you and the gay community. He's a dedicated Defender. Do you accept my apology, chocolate drop?" asked Loyd as I playfully glared at him.

"Of course I do... Now bring me up to speed on the mayhem that's brewing at headquarters."

"The Pink House is swamped with volatile Defenders inside the command center and outside the premises."

"Swamped, meaning what?" I asked while fiddling with the copper-colored zipper affixed to Loyd's properly pressed trousers.

"Swamped as in there's over two thousand armed LGBT affiliates on guard outside The Pink House and another two thousand or so armed Same-Sex Gladiators inside The Pink House. Your dynasty is primed to ration out justice to those that shun homosexuality. Hundreds of them are figuratively foaming at the mouth. The local cops are baffled and on edge by seeing the outstanding array of upscale weaponry that is being brandished and wielded. The National Guard and SWAT have been deployed to restore order and protect heterosexual citizens if violence ensues."

"Let me get this straight... You're telling me there's a grand total of four thousand or more armed openly gay men and women positioned outside and inside The Pink House?"

"Yep, that's exactly what I'm telling you. And to top it off, hundreds of LGBT members are taunting the local cops and the SWAT Unit by dauntlessly pointing loaded rifles at them. One brazen babe blatantly sicced her two bullmastiffs on the K-9 Unit. Dozens of transgendered teens from Deerfield, Lake Bluff and McHenry County showed up, with a chip on their shoulders. The picket signs they had in their possession, along with the Molotov cocktails, were comical yet monumental. Bisexual men and women exited luxury sedans clutching hand grenades and crossbows. Distraught lesbians exited tour buses and shuttle buses wielding samurai swords, gothic scimitars and submachine guns. Suburban same-sex parents exited their Volvo wagons and RVs carrying flamethrowers, nail guns and lit torches. Drag queens from surrounding cities exited their armored SUVs and modified riot trucks cradling sniper rifles, sabers, M-16s and AR-15s.

"The president held a live news conference forty minutes ago. He wore a mouse-colored suit. He assured the American people and the gay community that, if the National Guard is forced to engage in combat with LGBT insurgents, he will not sanction drone attacks on supporters of same-sex revolters."

CHAPTER EIGHTEEN— SAME-SEX DIVORCE

"No offense Mr. President, but it's been brought to my attention that a few of your cabinet members deemed it utterly inappropriate that you kept toying with your silk tie during the live press conference..."

"Fuck them," shouted the president while adjusting his pink silk tie. "They're always deeming things that I do inappropriate. Last week they found it inappropriate that I was watching the season premiere of the Lance Bass and Michael Turchin wedding special that premiered on the Oxygen Channel. The week before that, they deemed it inappropriate that my aviator and I were aboard Air Force One watching back-to-back episodes of Fashion Queens and Transparent. It's my prerogative to watch what I want to watch. So what, I enjoy watching Miss Lawrence, Bevy Smith and Derek J. assess and criticize the tacky attire that wealthy dudes and rich debutantes wear. You tell my cabinet that I deem it "inappropriate" and insubordinate that they continually gossip about me behind my back. You tell that bootlicker Sam that if I ever hear him make another lewd joke about the transgendered service men and women that serve this country, I'll have his badge and I'll personally have him exiled to a remote village in Cambodia. Also inform that brownnoser Jacob that if another person tells me he stated that I've got feminine qualities and a matronly swagger, he'll be dishonorably discharged from my cabinet and stripped of his diplomatic immunity. And you tell that freckle-faced harlot Joanne that if I get wind that she's tweeting biased remarks about my perspective on same-sex adoption, I'll tell the White House correspondents about the girl-on-girl liaisons she's had in Palm Springs and Aspen."

"Harness your emotions, Mr. President. It's foolish and fruitless to vent about your constituents. A lad of your status and stature must remain vigilant and stoic at all times."

"I concur," shouted the president after extracting his corncob pipe from its alloy case.

"Nice speech, honey," stated the first lady as she strolled into the drafting room. "It already went viral," she further stated after sitting on Dotson's lap. "I'm proud of you for not letting Congress and Homeland Security sway you into ordering a drone attack on those mourning homosexuals."

"This is America. They have a right to vent and take to the streets. They have a right to bear arms against the unseen entity that's killing off their associates and ambassadors. Many of those same-sex couples have been bullied most of their lives. A great deal of them have been sexually abused, verbally abused and physically abused. They're tired of being judged, ridiculed and shunned by their fellow Americans. This isn't a revolt you're witnessing, honey. This is the commencement of a sex war, the war of the century. The openly gay beings that dwell in America and other countries are fed up with society's perpetual disrespect toward the gay beings that reside in this country. The gay entities that are rooted in America are financially equipped to declare war on biased heterosexuals and limp-dick lawmakers.

"There's an indefinite number of gay people that live in the United States. They're becoming more dauntless and volatile by the hour. It's the year 2020, babe. The gays of this era will not tolerate the glares and despicable comments that people make about them and their kind. I personally commend the Defenders of Same-Sex Courtship for rallying their troops. America, and especially the critical citizens of Illinois, needs to witness the gay community coming together and fearlessly displaying a level of militia-like deportment."

"The Cook County and Lake County sheriffs have no idea how to deal with thousands of armed LGBT rebels that are chanting homosexual psalms," stated the first lady while she straightened out the president's pink tie.

"There's not a human on this planet that knows how to appease and calm down thousands of armed and emotional homosexuals that appear eager to participate in a gun fight with the National Guard and local authorities," shouted President Dotson after placing his corncob pipe back in its case. "If I sex war ensues, there'll be a great deal of casualties. The same-sex revolutionaries of this generation will be esteemed martyrs. Before deciding to hold a live press conference on this delicate matter, I attentively reviewed thirty-eight minutes of live video and audio footage of the armed and angry LGBT soldiers. And I must admit, the display of unity and unison was monumental and eerie. There was one dashing chap dressed in a salmon-colored mackintosh, clutching a damn flamethrower. The two lads to his left were dressed in pink cocktail dresses, toting M-16s."

"The most menacing of them all was the drag queen cradling the Gatling gun," shouted Dotson's message strategist, Dan Robinson.

"I disagree," shouted Dotson while running his fingers through the first lady's mahogany-colored dreadlocks. "I spotted a platoon of prissy young men wielding Slovenian sniper rifles. The scowls on their faces, along with the Kevlar vests they had on, put me under the impression that they were specifically wired to dispense affliction out to those that rudely oppose the openly gay lifestyle."

"The instant I spotted those transgendered teens brandishing hand grenades and crossbows, I properly understood that the gay community cannot and will not be bullied or eradicated," stated Dan while pouring himself and the president a glass of Belgian bourbon.

"During the live press conference, many of the gay radicals weren't receptive to what you had to say," stated the first lady, while delving through her Fossil purse for her prescription pain medication. "A great deal of them was clearly relieved to hear you promise that drone attacks will not be deployed."

"Surely you all don't think that a sexuality war is brewing?" asked Dan after handing Dotson his double-shot of bourbon.

"My intuition tells me that an all-out war may not ensue, but rumor has it that people that are in amorous allegiance with the LGBT lifestyle are covertly vengeful, venomous and vehement. With that being said, one can't help but be assured that these Defenders of Same-Sex Courtship will surely cause an array of catastrophic examples. So, in the near future, the up-and-coming prejudiced politicians, lazy lawmakers, and racist citizens of the United States will show esteem to those that are on the noble quest of obtaining a same-sex marriage certificate to regard and value the priceless sight of a same-sex couple that has the delightful dream of someday raising children that they adopted from gloomy orphanages, and to honor the unique individuals that enjoy flaunting their sexuality and their sexual preference."

"Hey, has anyone seen my bottle of Oxycontins? And my bottle of Percocets?" asked the first lady as Dan finished his cocktail.

"Maybe you left them in one of the thirteen tote bags that you donated to the battered women's shelter," stated President Dotson while nervously adjusting his rose gold cufflinks.

"Maybe... you've been foraging through my assortment of handbags, pilfering my prescription pills and self-medicating as usual," shouted the first lady while rising to her feet.

"Dan, can you excuse me and my petulant wife? The cessation of her fickle menstruation has her in a bitchy and pesky mood."

"How dare you speak down to me in front of one of your pawns?" shouted the first lady as Dan exited the Oval Office.

"How dare you accuse me of rummaging through your tacky tote bags and stealing your medication? Do I strike you as the type of commander that would filch your pills?"

"Yes, yes you do strike me as the type of congressional commander that would ransack a queen's purse and poach her pain pills. The pain medication I'm exclusively prescribed could never neutralize or soothe the guilt and shame that you're harboring... You are a halfwit husband. I'd rather eat some pussy than engage in a lovers' quarrel with you."

"You'd rather eat some pussy, huh?" asked President Dotson as he poured himself a double-shot of imported Singapore scotch. "Well, FYI First Lady, I'd rather watch you orally please a damsel than endure another night of your loud snoring."

"Fuck you," shouted the first lady while glaring at the shot glass of scotch.

"You're a witless wife. It's cunts like you that inspire men to seek companionship and validation with other men."

"You're a tasteless tyrant," yelled the first lady. "It's tools and dishonest jerks like you that incite females and give women the illuminating impetus to fish for and prowl after love, romance and partnership with other dames."

"You don't make me happy," shouted the president after gulping down the entire double-shot of scotch. "If you made me happy, maybe I wouldn't be entertaining the thought of sleeping with a dashing Swiss racecar driver that I met in Aspen at a millionaires-only ski resort."

"You're a sick son of a bitch," stated the first lady while removing her emerald-studded wedding ring. "I want a divorce," she further stated after flinging the ring at Dotson. "And just so you know, I'm having an affair. She's a petite princess from Trinidad. She understands me and treats me like a royal queen."

"That's phenomenal that you've managed to find a lover that isn't vexed by your hillbilly snoring and the fact that your vaginal cavity is often arid and frequently reeks of fermented smelts."

"Your cabinet and the US citizens that voted for you last year would be filled with horror and dismay to hear their prestigious Presbyterian president address his wife in such a malicious manner... I'm your wife, for Christ's sake. At all costs, I'm to be exalted and edified by you and your administration. I'm to be revered and always reverenced by you and your skirt-chasing constituents. It's treacherous, treasonous and downright transgressive how you behave toward me."

"Blah, blah, blah..." mumbled Dotson as Dan stormed into the Oval Office.

"I apologize for not knocking before entering, Sir, but we have a sinister situation. The Central Intelligence Agency just received substantiated evidence that Detective Stevenson IS INDEED being held against his will in the auditorium of the faggot fortress."

"Did you just refer to their command center as the FAGGOT fortress?" asked Dotson as he removed a bantam-size switchblade from his wool blazer pocket. "Listen here, messenger Dan. If I ever hear you utter the phrase faggot again, I'll personally drown you in my boyfriend's bathwater."

CHAPTER NINETEEN— OPENLY GAY

Outside The Pink House, the tension between the LGBT affiliates and law enforcement was now ultra-intense. The transgendered teens weren't at all intimidated by the presence of the National Guard. As the armed forces assembled their own militaristic margin around the perimeter of The Pink House, the teens brandished their hand grenades at them while bisexual brutes pointed rifles, rocket launchers and crossbows at them. The trained military operatives were given stern orders to ignore the teasing and taunting.

A few dozen Defenders had become bored with taunting, teasing and challenging the dudes dressed in SWAT gear. The gay gentlemen from Deerfield and Lake Bluff were ready to spill blood on same-sex soil. The drag queens were calm, cool and collected but their frequent snarls and growls insured their same-sex siblings and the skittish Cook County sheriffs that the monumental desire to rid America of the varmints that would love to see same-sex courting outlawed and banished from the galaxy were still being fed and validated. The lawless lesbians blew air-kisses at the female cadets while aiming their submachine guns at the cavalry of confederate canines that barked haphazardly.

"Shut those mongrel mutts up," shouted Sebastian as he and hundreds of his gay Spartans sashayed out of The Pink House. The dog leash that Sebastian was despotically holding was a restraining chain attached to the sapphire-studded metal collar that was illicitly clamped around Detective Stevenson's slender neck.

"Hey, that's one of our men," shouted a fellow from the K-9 Unit.

"Come and get him," shouted Sebastian as three of his transsexual confidantes screwed sleek suppressors onto their stolen Uzis.

"Captain Rogers, that's Detective Stevenson from our homicide division," shouted the K-9 Unit officer as Sebastian advanced toward an armored 1981 Z-28 Camaro that belonged to his mother's new girlfriend.

"You've got approximately twenty seconds to release Detective Stevenson," shouted Captain Rogers while calibrating the safety lever on his police-issued AR-15.

"Lower your tone and lower that rifle," shouted Sebastian, "before you're trampled by a squad of openly gay vindicators wearing glass slippers, combat boots and suede moccasins."

"Release Detective Stevenson," shouted a brawny operative cloaked in full body armor, cradling a limpid fiberglass riot shield.

"Or what?" shouted Megan as she activated her flamethrower and pointed it at one of the frantically barking K-9s.

"Are you okay? Detective Stevenson?" asked Captain Rogers as he gawked at the U-shaped aluminum staples that had recently been driven into his upper and bottom lip.

"These queers have stapled Stevenson's mouth shut," shouted a female officer that was carrying an iron battering ram.

"His urethra has been stapled shut as well," stated Sebastian as he handed the dog leash over to a narc standing next to a police cruiser.

"He's now no earthly good," shouted the hunk that purposely pointed his bazooka at a SWAT utility van. "He's unable to speak at the moment, but we're confident that the second those staples are manually dislodged, Mr. Stevenson will rant and rave about how paramount and earnest it is that the people of the United States start making a sincere effort to publically venerate same-sex courting and embrace the refreshing fact that the homosexuality culture is now and forever part of the planet's resilient ecosystem."

Promptly after being given the restraining chain that was affixed to the metal collar clasped around Stevenson's neck, Captain Rogers ushered the detective to an ambulance that was parked behind a salami-colored Audi S3.

As Captain Rogers and the severely injured Stevenson made their way over to the ambulance, an elderly lady armed with a Remington M-24 sniper rifle was making her way over to the roof of a coffee shop. The ultra-HD scope that was attached to the rifle wasn't as sleek and snazzy as the upscale silencer that was annexed to the snout of the weapon. The sixty-three-year-old woman reached the rooftop in a matter of minutes. This coffee shop belonged to her son and sat directly across from The Pink House. The elderly lady was pleased with the priceless vantage point that the roof rendered. While mounting the sniper rifle on a facilitation pedestal, she thought about the shoddy press conference that President Dotson had insincerely given.

"Same-sex marriage is an abomination," mumbled the senior citizen as she peered through the scope affixed to the rifle. The lens of the scope made the armed forces personnel and hostile homosexuals appear significantly closer than they actually were. Being masterful at paintballing, dart throwing and lazer tag, as well as the first person shooter video games that everyone wondered why she loved so much, the elderly dame was confident that she'd be able to quietly pick off a dozen or so abominable Defenders without being detected.

As she leveled the digital crosshairs on a fellow in pink snug-fitting fatigues, she thought about the tasteless liaison she had with a female lifeguard twenty-eight years ago. Before pulling the trigger, she thought about the inappropriate kissing and intense fondling they engaged in. She thought about her husband of sixteen years... and how he's currently having an affair with a male hip-hop mogul...

Just as her eyes filled with tears, she applied pressure to the trigger and the rifle coughed and jerked, sending an armor piercing projectile into the stomach of a gay lad wearing pink fatigues, clutching a sawed-off shotgun. The bullet entered his stomach and chipped two of his vertebra before it exited his lower back. The odd odor of ignited gunpowder and the surreal sight of old fashioned black gunpowder smoke appearing and dissipating enchanted the old lady. She wasted no time leveling the crosshairs on another queer and pulling the trigger. The bullet struck a middle-aged lesbian in the left collarbone and tore a hole through her flesh, leaving behind a void in her shoulder all at once. It was as if her shoulder had simply exploded. Her high-pitched screams alerted her squadron that they were under attack.

Just as the wounded lesbian sought cover behind a municipal fire truck, a redheaded freckle-faced transgendered teen extracted the safety pin from one of his hand grenades and hurled it at the crowd of K-9 Unit handlers. Three seconds later, the grenade exploded. The explosion ripped through the sound of gunfire to be heard alone. The grenade neutralized several canines and injured two K-9 officers. The shrapnel from the grenade struck Captain Rogers in the right shin just as the elder on the rooftop sent her third projectile into the face of a bisexual male clutching a curved Oriental sword.

Abruptly after the bullet struck the sword wielding bisexual in the cheek, an openly gay soccer dad overtly aimed his rocket launcher at a dozen National Guard troops, and without warning he fired an armor-piercing rocket at them. Immediately after firing the rocket launcher, a Cook County sheriff mowed him down using a recoilless M-16. As cops and LGBT affiliates exchanged gunfire, the senior perched on the rooftop aimed her rifle at a cat-eyed chap squatting beside a Z-28 Camaro, clutching a bazooka. The pink oxfords he had on insured the elder that he was an avid homosexual indulger, and that alone is why she sent a slug into his upper torso.

Sebastian coughed up four ounces of blood as he fell against the Camaro. Many of the Same-Sex Avengers charged at the SWAT Unit. As other Defenders flung grenades and lit Molotov cocktails at the Lake County sheriffs, the barrage of gunfire stemming from both parties left homosexuals and heterosexuals sprawled out in front of The Pink House.

Many officers and many LGBT members ran for cover and sought refuge behind the automobiles that peppered the premises. As murder and mayhem were being carried out in front of The Pink House, the sixty-three-year-old damsel was doing a poor job of dismantling her sniper rifle.

The Same-Sex Defenders that were dressed in full body armor stood their ground and fired round after round at the National Guard troops. The National Guard troops and other deputies cloaked in Kevlar body armor stood their ground as well. The National Guard troops were trained and primed for this level of intimate ground combat. Their nonchalance telegraphed the inhumane fact that euthanizing homosexuals was a chore they deemed fit for aspiring cadets and brave bounty hunters.

CHAPTER TWENTY— COMMUNITY

24 HOURS EARLIER...

"Where are we going, Carla?" asked Loyd while gazing at a photo of Sam Smith.

"We're headed to the orphanage, babe."

While en route to the Merryville Orphanage located on 18th and Montrose, I thought about the fatherless young girls and the motherless young boys that were currently being housed in the gloomy institution. I thought about the cold porridge they were served every morning and the broken toys they were given at Christmastime. I also thought about the years I spent in various foster homes, and the cold porridge I too was frequently served for supper, and the broken toys I received from strangers.

Unbeknownst to Loyd and our Cambodian chauffeur, I also thought about the inappropriate touching and fondling that I unjustly experienced while in DCFS custody. I somewhat understood that being introduced to oral sex and other sexual acts at the age of ten by a forty-year-old priest and staff members at the array of foster homes I resided in is primarily to blame for my zealous attraction to men of all ages and all nationalities. Being molested as a young boy by a slew of adult men and a few adult dames has shaped my perspective, heightened my sex drive and jaded my perception. Growing up motherless has a lot to do with the fact that I have such a ladylike disposition, yet the temper of a Cuban dictator. Growing up with no knowledgeable dad to raise and steer me is surely the reason why my temper even has a bad temper.

As the sedan came to an abrupt stop in front of the orphanage, I gazed over at the one man that sincerely loves me, the one man that validates my measly existence and values my plethora of shortcomings...

"Why are you staring at me?" asked Loyd after removing the pistol from my lap. "You must want me to shed these three hundred dollar trousers so you can have your way with me again."

"It's impolite to tease and taunt a sex kitten," I sternly stated. "The last time you made a cocky remark like that you found yourself fatigued, empty, limp and sprawled out on the kitchen floor, half-naked with your dick in one hand and my panties in the other hand..."

"I'm in no mood to banter with you, babe," whispered Loyd. "Let's ration out this cash to these parentless children and document their grateful smiles."

Loyd and I exited the sedan and made a beeline for the front entrance. The Merona tote bag I was carrying was filled with five-dollar bills – four hundred five-dollar bills to be exact. Every month on the eighth, Loyd and I would visit the orphanage and ration out bills to anyone able to give us any intelligence on same-sex divorce, same-sex marriage, same-sex lovers, openly gay people, gay advocates, gay trends, same-sex marriage licenses, etc. etc. The youth inside the orphanage eagerly looked forward to our visits. Many of them would do extensive research on LGBT data just to convey it to us. Although the majority of the information they shared with us was often grand intel that we were already aware of, we still felt a desire to pay them for the information out of courtesy.

We entered the parentless enclosure and were immediately greeted by an elderly security guard that smelled of cigarette smoke and Axe body spray.

"Hi Carla. What's up Loyd?"

"Good afternoon, Jeremy," stated Loyd while intentionally avoiding eye contact with the security guard.

"Hey Jeremy. Are the children in the gymnasium?" I anxiously asked after handing the cash-filled tote bag to Loyd.

"Yep," shouted Jeremy. "And they're armed with sacred intel about same-sex divorce that I personally helped them to extract from the tabloids and gossip blogs... So what's the scoop with you and Loyd? Are you two a couple or what? I overheard the children saying that you're gonna make an honest man out of Loyd someday..."

"Mind your business, Jeremy," shouted Loyd while glaring at me.

I ushered Loyd to the gymnasium before Jeremy found himself needing dentures and reconstructive lip surgery.

The very second we entered the gymnasium the kids began yelling gleefully and clapping synchronously. The standing ovation they gave us made my eyes water. These parentless kids made me feel royal and relevant.

After twenty seconds of enthusiastic and prolonged applause, I swaggered over to the podium. As silence fell over the gymnasium, the damsel in charge of the facility gave me a sincere salute and a sly wink that assured me that she wasn't at all threatened by my presence or envious of me. However, before addressing the orphans I couldn't help but notice that she gazed at Loyd as if he was a Hollywood heartthrob.

"Hi, boys and girls," I gleefully shouted after making a mental note to inform her later that Loyd was spoken for.

"Hi, Miss Carla," the kids shouted harmoniously as Loyd unzipped the tote bag.

"I've got cash. Who's got trustworthy data concerning LGBT?"

"I do! I do! I do!" shouted the children while frantically raising their small hands.

"You guys know the rules, only speak when I point to you, and after you verbally share the LGBT data, you're to make your way over to Loyd and he'll reward you for being astute and scholarly. David, step forward and share your LGBT data."

"Me and eight of my playmates have information concerning gay divorce," shouted David as he and eight of his pals stepped forward.

"Gay divorce, huh?"

"Yep, gay divorce," shouted a twelve-year-old girl named Janice.

"I'd first like to inform you and Loyd that on September 21, 1996, President Clinton signed the Defense of Marriage Act into law, defining marriage as the union of one man and one woman and making same-sex divorce a seriously messy affair."

"That's factual intel, David. Proceed over to Loyd so he can award you with some lunch money."

"Hi, Miss Carla," shouted Jamie as she bashfully stepped forward, clutching a wallet-size cue card. "I've got some factual intel as well," stated Jamie while gazing at the card in her hand.

"Let's hear it," shouted Loyd while adjusting the web cam apparatus.

"On September 13, 2004, a lesbian couple in Ontario became Canada's first same-sex divorcees. Initially, the application hit snags. While same-sex marriage was legal, Canadian divorce law hadn't caught up and still defined a spouse as "either of a man or a woman who are married to each other." A justice from the Ontario Superior Court rules that the definition of spouse is unconstitutional and the divorce goes through."

"That was very insightful, Jamie. Head over to Loyd to reap the fruits of your digest."

Thirteen-year-old Oliver stepped forward with the cockiness of an army Ranger. I listened intently, appreciating the eloquence of his speech.

"FYI Miss Carla, on April 4, 2005... four years after legalizing same-sex marriage, the Dutch government issues a report card on the institution. While the divorce rate for LGBT couples is on par with that for heteros, it seems that slightly more lesbians than gay men choose to split up..."

"Good job, Oliver."

As Oliver raced over to Loyd, Daphne stepped forward and spoke. "June 26, 2006. Two Spanish men who'd been married eight months became Spain's first same-sex couple to file for divorce. In seeking damages, one man claims that he gave up his modeling career and his dog-grooming business for love…"

"That intel is smothered in truth and sadness, Daphne. Good job."

"What's up, Miss Carla?" shouted Tiewan as he approached the podium.

"Hi, Tiewan. That grin on your face tells me that you've got LGBT data for sale."

"I sure do. And I want twenty dollars for the information, because last month your boyfriend only gave me ten dollars for the data I gave you guys on same-sex adoption."

"I'm not her boyfriend," shouted Loyd as he handed Daphne three five-dollar bills.

"I see the way you gaze at her when she's not looking," stated Tiewan.

"Do you have intel to share or not?" asked Loyd while fiddling with the heap of five-dollar bills.

"I've got intel, and I said I'd expect at least twenty dollars for this data."

"Let's hear it, hotshot," I firmly stated while peeping over at the now uncomfortable Loyd.

"On August 10, 2009 the National Enquirer reports that Rosie O'Donnell has split from wife Kelli Carpenter. O'Donnell blogged about marital woes but then, through her publicist, denies reports of the split – until, on her Sirius satellite radio show, a dog psychic gets her to admit that Carpenter actually moved out two years prior."

"And where did you find this information?" I asked while assessing his boyish dimples.

"A skirt-chaser never tells… Isn't that right, Loyd?" shouted Tiewan as he swaggered over to Loyd to collect his twenty dollars.

The next orphan to step forward was a fourteen-year-old girl that had the legs of a dancer and the posterior of a Vegas showgirl. She was attractive. While stepping forward she sucked in her stomach, adjusted her posture and batted her eyes at my Loyd. Seconds before she spoke, it dawned on me that the Daisy Duke shorts she had on were utterly improper attire for this parentless habitat.

"Although same-sex marriage is illegal in New York, state Supreme Court Justice Laura Drager agreed to let a lesbian couple who married in Canada file for divorce in the Empire State. In October 2008, New York grants its first divorce to a same-sex couple married elsewhere in the United States."

"That's sound intel, Tiara. I enjoyed listening to you speak."

"I've got data to share," stated a young boy that smiled at me in a way that made me feel pretty. As he stepped forward, I watched Tiara sashay over to Loyd and collect her ten dollars. The way she looked at my man annoyed me, yet I wasn't at all threatened by her video girl façade. Besides, I knew with certainty that my Loyd wasn't interested in warm pussy and young girls.

"Thomas Adkins and Wesley Nyberg – one of the first gay couples to wed in California in 2008 – separate and file for divorce thirteen days after their nuptials. Adkins, age fifty-five, tells a San Diego newspaper that he doesn't regret getting married. Also, three years after the landmark Goodridge v. Department of Public Health case led to the legalization of gay marriage in Massachusetts, plaintiffs Julie and Hillary Goodridge call it quits. Their divorce was finalized in 2009."

"I've got same-sex intelligence that'll astonish you and Mr. Loyd," shouted Howard as he stepped forward clutching an index card.

"The intel he has is data that he fleeced from Sean's footlocker," stated Jermaine.

"I'm academically savvy, Miss Carla. Boys of my caliber don't fleece data from their peers. This lad is a compulsive talebearer, a fatherless whistleblower of the highest order. Be advised, Miss Carla, that Angelique Naylor and Sabina Daly married in Massachusetts in 2004 and were granted a divorce in Texas, until Attorney General Greg Abbott intervenes, arguing that his state can't sanction a divorce for a marriage it considers invalid. Eleven months and several appeals later, a State Appellate Court rules that he was outside his jurisdiction."

Before I could compliment the information he shared, he made a dash toward Loyd to retrieve the bills Loyd was waving at him.

"Miss Carla, I've got LGBT info," stated Jermaine, "And let the record reflect that I'm no talebearer, and I'm no whistleblower. My dad is serving a life sentence in Stateville Prison due to the manufactured testimony of a renowned whistleblower. With that being said, I'd like to inform you and Mr. Loyd that on April 15, 2010, Melissa Etheridge split from her partner of nine years, actress Tammy Lynn Michaels. The news becomes tabloid fodder. Etheridge requests that Michaels not receive a dime in alimony, leading the actress to post these lines of poetry on her blog: "her broken promises / told to me by / headlines.""

"I'm impressed, Jermaine. I can tell you've done some noteworthy research to obtain that same-sex gossip."

After smiling at me, Jermaine marched over to Loyd to collect his awarded greenbacks.

"I'd like thirty pieces of silver for the privileged propaganda I'm about to divulge to you and Loyd," stated Maria in her theatrical British accent. "Eleven months after Argentina became the first Latin American country to legalize same-sex marriage, a lesbian couple, together for six years but married for only two months, files to become South America's first same-sex divorce statistic..."

As Maria spoke, I noticed that in her right hand was a painting of Peter Zupcofska. Rumor has it that Zupcofska was the country's preeminent gay divorce lawyer.

"What's with the painting?" I asked as Maria sauntered over to Loyd to receive her three five-dollar bills.

"The painting is for Mr. Loyd, "stated Maria as Loyd handed her fifteen dollars. "Since Mr. Loyd has made it abundantly clear that he's not your boyfriend, I now intend to give him this painting to remind him never to marry a dame that he can't tame."

Immediately after Loyd accepted the painting, I excused myself and made a beeline to the ladies room to powder my nose and collect my thoughts. During my stroll to the lavatory it became clear to me that Loyd would never come out of the closet with his sexuality, and never publicly proclaim and profess his love, adoration and commitment to me... Tears blotched my mink eyelashes and metallic eye shadow as I entered the ladies room.

Once inside, I stepped into one of the stalls to sulk and urinate. After hiking up my floral print dress and being sure to not actually sit on the porcelain toilet, several young ladies entered the powder room. From my vantage point I could see that all three women were wearing tacky strapless peep toe pumps. The make and model of their shoes was a sure sign that I was among gossipy gals that despised transgendered vixens that were virtuous and volatile. I stifled my sniveling and began quietly discharging urine into the basin.

"That Carla is something else," stated one of the women as I adjusted my panties. "She has some temerity to come to our place of work every month and hoggishly ration out cash to the residents that are able to acutely recite homosexual datum and same-sex statistics. The proprietor of this founding home is in egregious error for allowing her to come in and pay the children to study and embrace gay jargon, bisexual rhetoric, lesbian lingo and transgendered idiom."

Steam began coming out of my nose as I listened to the women slander me and the lifestyle I have wholeheartedly pledged my allegiance to.

"Did you all see the tacky-ass wig she wore last month?" asked one of the ladies as I stood upright and straightened out my dress.

"I didn't see it, but Catherine told me how messy it looked and how little Jermaine had to inform her that her wig was crooked."

"I don't like her. She's odd and narcissistic."

"That Pink Friday fragrance she wears causes me to sneeze..."

"What's up with that hunk that follows her like a puppy?"

"Oh, that's Loyd Stevenson. He's a homicide detective."

"I'd like to fuck him," shouted one of the chicks, just as I exited the stall.

"He's not attracted to cunts and skanks," I vexatiously stated. "I overheard the jealously-driven remarks you three stooges were making. It's bitches like you that sway legislative entities to veto same-sex marriage bills."

Before either of the ladies had a chance to vocalize a bitchy retort, I swiftly spit a mouthful of slightly alkaline fluid into the face of the woman that stood to my left, applying pure matte lipstick to her lips.

After rationally spitting in one woman's face, I rushed the bitch to my right and within seconds I had skillfully placed her in the rear naked choke. As I choked out the damsel, I glared at her cowardly colleagues as they stormed out of the powder room, screaming and yelling like two rape victims that had managed to elude their sadistic attacker...

CHAPTER TWENTY-ONE— HYPOCRITICAL HETEROSEXUALS

As Heather manually fed the capital-tallying machine a stack of hundred-dollar bills, she thought about the dearly departed James Avery. The fond thoughts about Mr. Avery were immediately suspended the moment that Kevin and Devin sashayed into the boardroom, hauling a laundry hamper filled with assorted bills.

"What's with the hamper?" asked Heather while inserting another stack of hundred-dollar bills into the mouth of the digitized money-counting apparatus.

"This hamper contains the spoils from this afternoon's comic book heist," stated Devin.

"What comic book heist?" asked Heather while documenting the tally of the last stack of bills she removed from the money-counting machine.

"Three nights ago, one of our pals that's into cosplay and Marvel comics contacted Devin and me, and conveyed to us that there's been several instances when a cosplay participant that's openly gay has been verbally bullied and repetitively ridiculed by a conspicuous comic book collector. We briefed Carla about the bullying and ridicule. She rewarded us with the tasteful task of administering punishment to the biased bully.

"Devin contrived a stratagem and was judicious and just. To make a long story short, we intercepted the hateful harasser exiting the Willis Tower, towing a sleek suitcase filled with antique comic books. After covertly taking the browbeating chump into our custody, we transported him to the dungeon. Once inside the dungeon, I gave him a fifteen-minute sermon on EQUALITY. After giving him the tedious exhortation, Kevin decided to dislocate both of his shoulders and intravenously add RODENT plasma to his bloodstream...

"As Kevin carried out the draconian chastisement and physical torment, I seized his personal effects and rummaged through his snazzy suitcase, and discovered an array of comic books. I contacted our black market fencer. He appraised the early edition comic books and offered us a small fortune for the Marvel comics. We accepted his offer. This should be fifty-six grand... Carla wants you and Walter to tally these greenbacks and see to it that every cent is donated to the Blinded Veterans Association."

"Where's the bully now?" asked Heather while dumping the heap of assorted bills onto the glass table. "I'd love to cram one of my bloody tampons down his throat and enlighten him on the significance of EQUALITY."

"Carla insisted that we chain him to a city dump truck so the Department of Streets and Sanitation can contact the cops and his next-of-kin."

"I'm tired," stated Heather while manually putting the assorted bills in neat, equally sized stacks. "I've been up since three a.m. tallying this capital, which Loyd allegedly fleeced from a trap house that belonged to a homophobic cartel member who was involved in trafficking firearms from suburban areas to the inner city."

"The other night I had a dream I fucked Loyd in our hot tub," whispered Devin while winking at Kevin.

"Keep your voice down," shouted Heather, "because if Walter or Sharon hear you making vulgar comments about fucking Loyd, they'll surely inform Carla that you're interested in fucking her fiancé. I believe he wants to sleep with me..." whispered Heather. "If Carla wasn't dangerously in love with him, I would have put this pussy at his disposal months ago."

"I like Loyd," stated Kevin. "I think he's perfect for our commander. He keeps her on an even keel, he's obviously making love to her on a daily basis, he's overtly kind to her and he's clearly in love with her. It befuddles me that he has yet to come out of the closet."

"He's a cop, for Christ's sake," shouted Devin. "His colleagues would surely ostracize him the instant he tells them that he's gay and engaged to a transgendered volatile vixen that's the commander-in-chief of a legion of prissy pirates and Same-Sex Spartans... He feels that coming out would tarnish his reputation and soil his badge."

"The dick must be intense and phenomenally unrivaled," shouted Devin, "because Carla has never been a fan of sleeping with closet-dwellers and ashamed gay men. It's never been her forte. But Loyd comes along and covertly woos her..."

"Loyd has majestic qualities, but at the end of the day he's ashamed to admit to his family and friends that he's harmoniously in alliance with the homosexual way of life. Until he comes out of the closet, I will always view him as a gutless hypocrite, a king that isn't worthy to drink Carla's bathwater, a spineless playboy that has no problem seducing a man behind closed doors but has a serious problem with kissing that same man in public... If I were Carla, I wouldn't put up with him or his closet games. I'd trade him in for a cocky chap that'll kiss me in public and flaunt our relationship around town."

"Cut the guy some slack," shouted Heather. "He'll eventually go public with his sexuality. Even you needed time and coaxing out of the closet."

"I didn't needing coaxing," stated Kevin. "I needed assurance that the gay community would provide me with provisions and refuge when my parents cut me off."

"I've got the intuition of a royal princess," shouted Devin, "and my intuition tells me that Loyd will come out of the closet sometime next week. He's a sound fellow. He's thoroughly aware that the relationship he has with Carla and us will soon go sour if he doesn't barge out of the closet soon with a set of his and his wedding bands and a bullhorn to facilitate the announcement that he's gay and gracious."

"Besides being tall, dark and dashing, what else does Carla find so bewitching about Loyd? Because it takes more than a big dick, a skillful tongue and a protective spirit to sweep Carla off her feet."

"One must be mindful that the heart wants what it wants," stated

Heather. "Carla sees things in Loyd that we're unable to see. And to top it off, he's very knowledgeable in matters concerning LGBT and same-sex courtship. Last week I witnessed him rubbing Carla's feet for an entire hour. And during the amorous foot rub, he conveyed to her that he has a pal named George Sears that's an executive director of the Williams Institute at the UCLA School of Law, which tracks gay and LGBT demographics and legal trends. He mentioned that his pal expects that half of the estimated sixty five thousand same-sex couples living together in New York will marry in the next three years, mirroring the rate seen in Massachusetts. He further stated that many of those unions wouldn't last, due to the fact that the projected rate of gay divorce is fifty percent, on par with that of straight couples. He then admitted to being invited to three gay weddings the year gay marriage was legalized in Boston. Carla listened quietly as Loyd told her about a hotshot named Ross D. Levi, an executive director of the Empire State Pride Agenda and Foundation. Rumor has it the Foundation was instrumental in making same-sex marriage happen in New York. He went on to say that he personally believes that same-sex couples have not internalized the fact that now, if things don't work out, the state has something to say about it.

"Although divorce is never mentioned as part of the gay marriage media blitz, men like Zupcofska and his ilk are convinced that same-sex marriage is similar to traditional marriage – and the idea of wealthy gays trading in their spouses for a hot Brazilian stallion hews closely to the time-honored tradition of a midlife crisis and trophy wife. It's still separate and unequal in the eyes of the US government…"

"I hate to interject but I've heard Loyd tell our commander that the 1996 Defense of Marriage Act (DOMA) says that the feds needn't recognize same-sex couples who are legally married in their home states. Nineteen years later, the cultural lines have become blurrier – even some tea partiers decry the law for the way it infringes on states' rights."

"In February, President Dotson said his administration would no longer defend the constitutionality of DOMA," shouted Heather.

"But it remains on the books. And even if the act is repealed, thirty-seven states have laws that define marriage as a union of one man and one woman. And each state is different. This means an ever-changing legal landscape awaits those entering into a gay marriage, as well as those exiting one…"

"Divorce is supposed to make life – for the state, for lawyers, for ex-spouses – easier," stated Devin as he crammed a wad of bills into the mouth of the capital-counting contraption.

"But thanks to DOMA and a lack of precedent, the tangle of custody issues, estate planning and tax codes will only grow thornier – and as more gay couples wrestle with what it means to end a state-sanctioned union, the emotional fallout will be greater, too. More storybook gay marriages means more soap opera divorces... All of which is of course good news for Zupcofska..."

"Who the hell is Zupcofska?" asked Walter as he sashayed into the boardroom carrying a crate filled with various silencers and boxes of high-caliber ammunition.

"Shame on your for not knowing who Peter Zupcofska is," stated Devin. "He's a sly shark that's fashioned himself into a pit bull gay divorce lawyer. He took his first gay breakup case in the mid-eighties, long before gay marriage was a legal hope, much less a reality... Much of his work is prenup or cohabitation agreements, although there have been a few cases that came out of left field, such as that of the two U.S. soldiers on leave from duty in a combat zone, who married in Massachusetts to avoid a stop-loss order that would have sent them back into harm's way. They claimed residency at a Boston hotel, got hitched, and both expected to be discharged under Don't Ask Don't Tell. Instead, the military called their bluff (no one in the platoon believed these two were actually involved) and they went back to combat duty. One of these not-actually-gay grunts came from a prominent family, and they were adamant that his sham marriage not following him through life... Zupcofska was brought in to make this gay marriage of convenience disappear, expunging it from Massachusetts records."

"Doesn't Zupcofska have a position at a blue-chip law firm in Boston?" asked Kevin as Walter sat the crate of silencers on the glass table next to the various money-counting machines.

"Yep. He's a partner at Burns and Levinson," stated Heather. "My ex claims to have seen him in the Bahamas when she and Carla went on a gay cruise last summer. She stated that he had good skin, a full head of hair, and a lilting Boston accent. Rumor has it that he and his hussy share a five-thousand-square-foot house on Cape Cod, and that he has a love of fur coats and gold jewelry. He's presided over all kinds of same-sex breakup horror stories. He's done a prenup for a gay couple with half a billion dollars in assets, he co-wrote the Boston Bar's Amicus Brief for the Goodridge v. Department of Public Health case – which legalized gay marriage in Massachusetts seven years ago – perhaps cementing his bona fides in Boston's gay circles. Just two years after the lesbian Goodridge couple won their landmark decision in the Massachusetts Supreme Court, their marriage fractured. They separated and, three years later, filed for divorce."

"You said all that to say what?" asked Walter as he adjusted the straps on his Giuseppe six-inch heels.

"Same-sex marriage is about the right to stand up in front of your family and associates and proclaim your love for someone of the same gender, and to have the state sanction that committed union..."

CHAPTER TWENTY-TWO— DISCRIMINATION

While manually unclasping her own leopard-print bra, Sharon coquettishly straddled her girlfriend. Her girlfriend was a heartbroken soccer mom that Sharon met at Wal-Mart eighty-six days ago. Her name was Ebony. She was the mother of four bashful boys that spent countless hours gaming online. With the four boys away at soccer practice, Sharon decided that today would be the day that she taught Ebony the art of eating pussy... Unbeknownst to Sharon, Ebony was introduced to pussy-eating thirteen years ago and was utterly proficient at orally pleasing a woman and sexually pleasing herself...

"Have you watched the news today?" asked Sharon after tossing her bra onto the nightstand.

"Earlier today I watched six minutes of C-SPAN," stated Ebony as she ran her left thumb across Sharon's right nipple. "A Michigan judge strikes down state's gay marriage ban."

"You're a news junkie," whispered Sharon as she began unbuttoning Ebony's silk blouse.

"The last bitch that called me a news junkie found herself blindfolded while eating fresh pussy for three hours," whispered Ebony as she slid two of her fingers into Sharon's moist love tunnel.

"I've got a pierced tongue that's indefatigable and inexhaustible. Therefore, the sheer threat or mere notion of being blindfolded while orally toying with some fresh pussy for three hours does sound a bit fun..."

"Michigan's ban on gay marriage is unconstitutional," stated Sharon while slowly gyrating her hips. "... A federal judge said Friday as he struck down a law that was widely embraced by voters a decade ago–"

"That's not the latest in a recent series of decisions overturning similar prohibitions across the country," shouted Ebony as she eased a third finger into Sharon's now pulsating pussy. "US District Judge Bernard Friedman released his thirty-one-page ruling exactly two weeks after a rare trial that mostly focused on the impact of same-sex parenting on children." As Sharon purposely leaked warm cum onto Ebony's three manicured fingers, she conveyed to her lover that supporters of same-sex marriage believe the Michigan ban was at least partly the result of animosity toward gays and lesbians, and how many Michigan residents have religious convictions whose principles govern the conduct of their daily lives and inform their own viewpoints about marriage. "Nonetheless, these views cannot strip other citizens of the guarantees of equal protection under the law."

"I'm about to cum," shouted Sharon as her nipples hardened and her left leg twitched, trembled and semi-stiffened.

"Attorney General Bill Schuette said he would immediately ask a federal appeals court to freeze Friedman's decision and prevent same-sex couples from marrying while he appeals the case."

"That biased attorney general seems to have political beef with those in favor of same-sex courtship," stated Sharon after climaxing for the fourth time that day. "My cousin Duane Gholston is a charming fellow that supports same-sex marriage," whispered Sharon as Ebony sucked her right breast. "He believes that marriage entitles you to a history of laws, to a financial and custodial framework to tie two people's fortunes "in every sense" together and to separate them with dignity. The right to enter a marriage fairly and legally is something the estimated four million gays in America are fighting for."

"Has Carla met your cousin Duane?" asked Ebony.

"She met him once and was impressed with his perspective on the evolutionary process of same-sex marriage. I vividly recall him expressing to Carla that gay breakups are every bit as heated as the divorces of straight couples. In same-sex divorces you have two uncompromising male egos or two female egos to contend with. It's very often a "War of the Roses" situation... It's "he said – he said" and "she said – she said." According to estimates by New York state officials, same-sex marriage – legalized this summer in a stunning late-night victory courtesy of Governor Andrew Cuomo – will bring $391 million to the state economy over the next three years. But lost amid the talk of all that loot is the windfall of gay divorce."

"You've killed my vibe with all this palaver about same-sex divorce and gay marriage."

"Conversing about LGBT affairs isn't idle chatter," shouted Ebony, "it's fruitful dialogue that'll edify you and enrich your perception... Such discussions should stimulate you and your lusty libido."

"This is the year 2020, a watershed moment in gay rights. Same-sex marriage is now legal in many states, plus Washington, DC and Canada, and soon New Jersey. And Maryland will fall in line next. And a movement in California is afoot to get a same-sex marriage initiative on the ballot soon. There are twelve more states with either domestic partnership laws or civil unions on the books that recognize gay marriages performed in other states. And for the first time in our nation's history, a Gallup poll shows that more than fifty percent of Americans believe same-sex marriage should be a legal right.

"Among eighteen- to thirty-four-year-olds, that number jumps to seventy percent. In the first four months that same-sex marriage was legal in California, before the passage of Prop 8 overturned that decision, more than sixteen thousand same-sex couples wed. I properly understand that gay marriage is the social topic of the moment," shouted Sharon. "But FYI my love, I came to this love nest of yours to be orally penetrated. If I wanted to engage in LGBT discourse, I would have spent the afternoon at The Pink House, listening to Carla and Sebastian converse about the outstanding significance of EQUALITY and same-sex courting. Every now and then I need a break from conversations that revolve around homosexuality. Last night I endured two hours of listening to Loyd go on and on about his hypothesis on the relationship that Neil Patrick Harris and his boyfriend David have. He mentioned that just because Neil and David will soon be able to marry in New York doesn't mean they're planning a wedding."

"Perhaps the prospective Mr. and Mr. Doogie Howser are wise to wait until the laws are sorted out. I read online that Florida doesn't recognize same-sex marriages from other states."

"Where are my panties?" asked Sharon while retrieving her bra from the nightstand.

"Your panties are dangling from the chandelier," shouted Ebony while smelling the vaginal secretion that varnished three of her fingers.

CHAPTER TWENTY-THREE— GAY BULLYING

"With gay divorce, the worst in humanity comes out," shouted Jessica as she placed eight pounds of shredded filet mignon in front of her female bullmastiff. "As a businesswoman, I'm starting to realize that I must become culturally sensitive to the gay lifestyle. More than half of the gay couples I know have open relationships... or geographically based monogamy. They frown on such behavior in Boston, but they'll go to South Beach and fool around. That's less common with lesbians, but they have their own issues. Everyone does.

"A gay divorce is, after all, more than a separation of assets. It's an emotional and instantly recognizable point of closure – a pockmarked period at the end of a sentence. Gay men and gay women want the catharsis of being able to spill their guts in a deposition, to say all the awful things you did to me, and all the grand things I was doing for you that you never appreciated."

"Are you talking to your dogs again?" asked Josh as he entered the wine cellar carrying a box that contained seventy-two ounces of pre-capsulated molly, three digital scales, a miniature blender and two cellphones.

"It comforts me to converse with my dogs about the adversity and cyber-capital the gays seem to effortlessly attract."

"It's silly and unhealthy to open a dialogue with vicious pit bulls," shouted Josh as he placed the box next to a bottle rack.

"My dogs may be savage and dangerous, but they're my pals," shouted Jessica as she placed three eight-ounce steaks in front of her male bullmastiff. "These dogs are my protectors, my confidantes. They're both supremely subordinate. They enjoy listening to my thoughts, not to mention they understand the warranted hate I have toward gay people and the contempt I have toward Carla and the vexatious Defenders of Same-Sex Courtship."

"A cunt like Carla and the Defenders of Same-Sex Courtship shouldn't even be on your RADAR," shouted Josh. "She's a stud that's aspiring to become a modern-day Rosa Parks. She's beneath you. She's a harmless black sheep, dressed in wolf's clothing. She'd ingest elephant semen and falcon urine if it guaranteed her that she'd develop a menstrual cycle."

"I see now... you're oblivious to the amount of revenue she's RAKING in daily. Unbeknownst to you and every other swinging dick in America, Miss Carla has miraculously mutated into the most powerful damsel in America. Rumor has it that this cunt extracted 1.3 million dollars out of her personal account and used every penny to purchase the following fallen pioneers new granite tombstones: Sherman Hemsley, Rock Hudson, Rosa Parks, Coretta Scott King, Malcolm X, Joan Rivers, and James Avery."

"Surely you don't expect me to believe that a transgendered punk that grew up with dirt under his fingernails took 1.3 million dollars of his own capital and upgraded the headstones of the dearly departed trailblazers?"

"As noble and grand as these deeds are, they're minor compared to the missionary work she and her companions have carried out using their time, cash and resources. She's notable in West Hollywood for kidnapping biased billionaires that despise people of the gay community, and extorting them out of millions of dollars, and using the spoils to combat famine and poverty in remote villages like Sudan, Mongolia and Laos."

"She sounds like a female Robin Hood," stated Josh, right before exiting the wine cellar.

As Josh exited the wine cellar, Jessica began chatting with her two bullmastiffs again. The two sapphire- and spike-studded dog collars that sat on her lap were trinkets she intended to give to the hounds for being loyal listeners.

"That Josh has the perception of an eel," shouted Jessica. Her two mastiffs barked synchronously, assuring their master that they affirmed her notions of Josh.

"I'm also certain that Josh has no clue that the Federal Government doesn't recognize same-sex divorce. Settlements create a tax minefield. In a heterosexual divorce, the transfer of assets isn't a taxable event, but when a gay couple divorces, transferred assets are taxed as gifts, often at up to fifty percent, or may be subject to capital gains penalties. Likewise, alimony payments for heterosexual divorcees are tax deductible, but in a gay split they can be taxed as gifts."

"I find it odd and comical that you converse with those dogs as if they're your pupils," stated Josh as he reentered the wine cellar, clutching a 30.06-hunting rifle.

"In a way, they are my placid pupils. I was just enlightening them on same-sex custody issues. I advise all same-sex couples to legally adopt their spouse's children – even if they live in a state that recognizes gay marriage. It's the issue of portability."

"They're dogs, babe. I'm sure they have no desire to hear about homosexuality. Last week, while en route to Miami to pick up sixteen pounds of high-quality kush, you spent forty minutes conveying to them that DOMA is steamrolling states' rights, saying that the federal government won't recognize gay marriage but also that no state is compelled to recognize another state's sanctioning of it."

"FYI Josh, a dog and every other breathing entity needs to know that if a same-sex couple wed in New York, move to Florida and want to divorce, they will likely find themselves in a legal morass. Florida can't legally end a marriage it never recognized. So one half of the couple will have to establish residency in a state where gay marriage is legal."

"I've got a question," stated Josh after putting the rifle into a closet. "Let's say I'm a foreign national. Can I marry an American man, get citizenship, and then split up?"

"That's a good question," shouted Carla as the male mastiff playfully gnawed at Josh's lemur-colored sandals. "The federal government – not the states – issues green cards, meaning that thanks to DOMA, gay green card marriage is an impossibility. Gay would-be immigrants looking to remain in the country will have to find lonely cash-starved ladies to marry them. There have been a number of heartbreaking stories of gay marriages with non-green cardholders that resulted in the noncitizen being forced to leave. And executing a gay divorce from abroad can involve even more hassles than doing so across state lines."

"It's cute and peculiar that you're ravenously abreast of LGBT developments," stated Josh. "You should become an advocate for transgender marriage. And write an epic tale about Carla and how she transitioned from dude to damsel. You can explain to readers how Carla's marriage to a local detective and their commitment to raising their adopted orphans represent the true meaning of love. You can give a digest on how their bond goes beyond sexual identity or orientation." As Josh sarcastically suggested that Jessica become a gay advocate, thoughts about commanding her two mastiffs to chase him into the nearest closet crossed her mind.

"Do I strike you as the type of bitch that's interested in becoming a gay advocate? I'm interested in power and cyber-capital. I'm interested in the ruby-encrusted pedestal that Carla has been placed on. I'm interested in building myself a proverbial empire that's a replica of Carla's. I'm interested in infiltrating her dynasty and fucking that cop that's always following her around."

"That cop is a local homicide detective. Rumor has it that he's her personal bodyguard," stated Josh after opening a bottle of champagne.

"I wouldn't give a rat's ass if he was her personal servant. I intend to bless him with some of this wet-ass pussy the moment I cross paths with him."

"What if he's not a fan of wet pussy?" asked Josh.

"Cops are addicted to wet pussy and fresh doughnuts. My sources tell me that his name is Detective Loyd Stevenson and that he's currently investigating a tragedy in the suburbs that involves nine teenagers committing suicide after being bullied. Four of the nine dead were either gay or perceived as such by other kids, and reportedly bullied... The tragedies come at a national moment when gays being bullied is on everyone's lips."

"A devastating number of gay teens across the country are in the news for killing themselves," stated Josh after taking a gulp of champagne straight from the bottle.

"Suicide rates among gay and lesbian kids are frighteningly high, with attempt rates four times that of their straight counterparts. Studies show that one third of all gay youth have attempted suicide at some point (versus thirteen percent of hetero kids) and that internalized homophobia contributes to suicide risk.

"Against this supercharged backdrop, the Anoka-Hennepin School District finds itself in the spotlight not only for the sheer number of suicides, but because it is accused of having contributed to the death toll by cultivating an extreme anti-gay climate. LGBTQ students don't feel safe at school. They're made to feel ashamed of who they are. They're bulled and there's no one to stand up for them, because teachers are afraid of being fired. The Southern Poverty Law Center and the National Center for Lesbian Rights have filed a lawsuit on behalf of five students, alleging the school district's policies on gays are not only discriminatory, but also foster an environment of unchecked anti-gay bullying. Carla and the Defenders of Same-Sex Courtship have begun a civil rights investigation as well..."

CHAPTER TWENTY-FOUR— GAY ADVOCATES

Catilina Ortega gazed at the two men cuddling on the park bench. Her gaze was filled with awe and envy. She didn't quite understand how two men dressed in cheap suits and cute slippers could find love and romance on this planet, when love and romance had been utterly impossible for her to locate and obtain...

Curious to know what it is that gay lovers converse about, Catilina strolled over to the park bench and sat down next to the gay couple. The two men issued each other Eskimo kisses as Catilina made herself comfortable. Her abrupt presence didn't at all startle or interrupt the amorous men. Catilina opened up her laptop and pretended to surf the Internet as she eavesdropped on their conversation.

"I love you, babe," whispered one of the men.

"I love you back," stated the other fellow while trying to shove his right hand down the front of his boyfriend's trousers.

"Quit being a naughty wolf," stated the man that wasn't allowing his mate to insert his talons down his trousers. "How was your meeting with the Defenders of Same-Sex Courtship?" asked the fellow guarding the front of his trousers.

"It was eerie and monumental. As you know, the meeting took place at The Pink House. Carla and her charitable cabinet were present. A feminine fellow by the name Sebastian allowed me to address the Defenders. I raised the issue about the madness and the gay teens being bullied at Anoka-Hennepin School. I informed Carla that the school district declined to comment on any specific incidences but denies any discrimination, maintaining that its broad anti-bullying policy is meant to protect all students. I also mentioned to Carla that the pompous superintendent, David Carlton had the nerve to say that his district is not homophobic and to be vilified for being so is very frustrating.

"Carla and her cabinet were appalled that Mr. Carlton blames right-wingers and gay activists for choosing the area as a battleground, describing his district as the victim in this fracas... That Carlton character is an insensitive weasel. That son of a bitch had the balls to say that same-sex couples are using kids as pawns in this political debate. I find that statement abhorrent.

"Located a half hour north of Minneapolis, the thirteen sprawling towns that make up the Anoka-Hennepin School District – Minnesota's largest, with thirty-nine thousand kids – seems an unlikely place for such a battle. It's a soothingly flat one-hundred-seventy-two-square-mile expanse sliced by the Mississippi River, where woodlands abruptly give way to strip malls and then fall back to placid woodlands again. And the landscape is dotted with churches. The district, which spans two counties, is so geographically huge as to be a sort of cross-section of America itself. For years, the area has also bred a deep strain of religious conservatism. At churches like First Baptist Church of Anoka, parishioners believe that homosexuality is a form of mental illness caused by family dysfunction, childhood trauma and exposure to pornography – a perversion curable through intensive therapy... It's a point of view shared by their congresswoman Monica Bachmann, who has called homosexuality a form of "SEXUAL DISFUNCTION" that amounts to PERSONAL ENSLAVEMENT.

"Although the SKANK Monica doesn't live within Anoka-Hennepin's boundaries anymore, she has a dowdier doppelganger there in the form of anti-gay crusader Barb Gladstone, a bespectacled grandmother with lemony-blond hair that she curls in severely toward her face. Gladstone is a former district Spanish teacher and a long-time researcher for the MFC who has been fighting gay influence in local schools for two decades, ever since she discovered that her nephew's health class was teaching homosexuality as normal.

""That really got me on a journey," she said in a radio interview. When the Anoka-Hennepin District's sex-ed curriculum came up for reevaluation, Bachmann and four like-minded parents managed to get on the review committee. They argued that any form of gay tolerance in schools is actually an INSIDIOUS means of promoting homosexuality – that openly discussing the matter would encourage kids to try it, turning straight kids gay."

"I wouldn't be surprised if Carla has Monica, Barb, those parishioners and Mr. Carlton skinned alive and force-fed cat poop..."

The sheer mention of Carla's name annoyed Catilina. She gritted her teeth as one of the men boasted about how attractive and eloquent in speech Carla is...

"I don't mean to chime in on you all's conversation but I've got pals in Washington, DC that are "defending marriage" by lobbying for anti-gay legislation," stated Catilina while giving the gay couple an unobstructed view of the Ruger that rested in the suede shoulder holster that once belonged to a CIA operative. "And fighting gay tolerance in public schools under the guise of preserving parental authority – reasoning that government-mandated acceptance of gays undermines the traditional values taught in Christian homes. My colleagues wrote a memo to the Anoka-Hennepin School Board concluding, "The majority of parents do not wish to have their children taught that the gay lifestyle is a normal acceptable alternative." Surprisingly, the six-member board voted to adopt the measure by a four-to-two majority, even borrowing the memo's language to fashion the resulting district-wide policy, which pronounced that within the health curriculum, "HOMOSEXUALITY" not be taught or addressed as a normal, valid lifestyle. The policy became unofficially known as "NO HOMO PROMO" and passed unannounced to parents and unpublished in the policy handbooks."

"Your pals may soon find themselves in Carla's torture chamber, groveling and whining for amnesty," stated one of the gay men as he extracted a .22 Derringer from the Dior fanny pack that was clasped around his waist.

"So your cowardly colleagues are the pencil pushers that gave birth to the NO HOMO PROMO, huh? Their principals told most teachers about it. Carla and our cohorts say it had a chilling effect and teachers became concerned about mentioning gays in any context. Discussion of homosexuality gradually disappeared from classes. If you can't talk about it in any context, which is how teachers interpreted the district policies, kids internalize that to mean that being gay must be shameful and wrong and that has created a climate of fear and repression and harassment."

"Homosexuality is a complex phenomenon," stated Catilina as she glared at the gay man clutching the small Derringer. "There's never any one pat reason to explain why a boy is sexuality attracted to another boy or why dames are sexually attracted to damsels... Suicide is also a complex phenomenon. No one can rationally explain why gay teens kill themselves."

CHAPTER TWENTY-FIVE— SAME-SEX AVENGERS

"Good afternoon, Mr. President. My name is Jerry Gaines. I'm an openly gay hands-on dad, and I'd like to share a story with you and the first lady..."

"Does the tale involve wizardry and mystical creatures?" asked President Dotson as the interior of his nostril itched and repeatedly twitched.

"No, Sir... Mr. President, the story is about a gay teen that killed himself," stated Jerry as a member of the security detail handed the president a silk handkerchief to combat his flared, runny nose.

"Is this a fiction or nonfiction story?" asked the first lady.

"It's a factual story that I'm sure you and your husband will enjoy," shouted Jerry.

"We're all ears," shouted a member of Dotson's cabinet.

"The summer before Justin Aaberg started at Anoka High School, his mother asked, "So, are you sure you're gay?" Justin, a slim, shy fourteen-year-old who carefully swept his blond bangs to the side, studied his mom's face. "I'm pretty sure I'm GAY," he answered softly, then abruptly changed his mind. "Whoa, whoa, whoa, wait!" he shouted – out of character for the quiet boy – "I'M POSITIVE. I am gay," Justin proclaimed.

"OK," Tammy Aaberg nodded. "So, just because you can't get him pregnant doesn't mean you don't need to use protection." She proceeded to lecture her son about safe sex while Justin turned bright red and beamed. Embarrassing as it was to get a sex talk from his mom, her easy affirmation of Justin's orientation seemed like a promising sign as he stood on the brink of high school. Justin was more than ready to turn the corner on the horrors of middle school – especially on his just-finished eighth grade year, when Justin had come out as gay to a few friends, yet word had instantly spread, making him a PARIAH.

"In the hall one day, a popular jock had grabbed Justin by the balls and squeezed, sneering, "You like that, don't you?" That assault had so humiliated and frightened Justin that he'd burst out crying, but he never reported any of his harassment. The last thing he wanted to do was draw more attention to his sexuality. Plus, he didn't want his parents worrying. Justin's folks were already overwhelmed with stresses of their own: swamped with debt, they'd declared bankruptcy and lost their home to foreclosure, so Justin had kept his problems to himself. He felt hopeful that things would get better in high school, where kids were bound to be more mature.

""There'll always be bullies," he reasoned to a friend, "but we'll be older, so maybe they'll be better about it."

"But Justin's start of the ninth grade in 2009 began as a disappointment. In the halls of Anoka High School, he was BULLIED, called a "faggot" and shoved into lockers. Then, a couple of months into the school year, he was stunned to hear about Sam Johnson's suicide, though Justin hadn't known her, and of the way she'd been taunted for being butch. Justin tried to keep smiling. In his room at home, Justin made a brightly colored paper banner and taped it to his wall. Scrawled across the banner was a profound phrase: "Love the Life you Live – Live the Life you Love.""

Gravity pulled a single tear out of the president's left tear duct and it descended down his cheek. Dotson dried his left eye as the first lady cynically yawned and gazed at her own reflection in the wallet-size mirror that was affixed to her iPhone.

"How ladylike and tasteful of you to yawn and scrutinize your new nose job while this lad is giving us a verbal synopsis of a traumatic tale," shouted the president while glaring at the first lady.

"Don't patronize me in front of your inebriated cabinet," shouted the first lady.

"It would be wise to gag that glamorous nag," whispered the vice president while glancing down at the crystal-encrusted Cartier that encircled his left wrist.

"It's taboo and outlandish that you allow your wife to address us and talk down to us as if we're mischievous minions," shouted Madam Secretary.

"She's ratchet and messy," stated Dotson while servicing his runny nose. "We must be mindful that she grew up entitled, and that her aristocratic foster parents didn't have the diplomatic decency to send her to a preparatory etiquette institute."

"Fuck you," shouted the first lady as she stormed out of the theatre room.

"She has the temperament of a scorned harlot," stated Dotson as he placed her GoJane tote bag on his lap. "Pardon her behavior. My wife doesn't respond well to candid dialogue that involves homosexual jargon. She's a cynical damsel that'll soon be replaced. Since the abrupt cessation of her menstruation she's been indecisive and quite bitchy. And for the record, it's been quite a spell since I've awarded her any dick or affection..."

"Mr. President... This isn't the time nor the place to rave about your wife's sour shortcomings," stated the vice president, just as Dotson began rummaging through the first lady's tote bag.

"I'm the President of the United States," shouted Dotson. "I can rant about my spouse's snooty attitude and her evident imperfections at my leisure. Besides, it's healthy for a king to vent to his comrades about his queen..."

"Mr. President, you have a call on line seven," shouted Madam Secretary.

"Did the caller identify himself?" asked Dotson as he pulled two bottles of prescription pain pills from the tote bag.

"Although the caller didn't identify himself, I'm certain it's a liaison from the Anoka-Hennepin School Board..."

"Tell them I'm in a meeting," whispered Dotson as he covertly placed the two bottles of pills in the front right pocket of his Burberry linen trousers.

"Eluding this call will surely be egregious, Mr. President."

"Tell the caller to call back in thirty minutes or so," stated Dotson.

"I want this fellow to tell us another tale about a gay teen being bullied and ridiculed... Can my constituents and I hear another story that involves a gay teen being unjustly bullied?"

"I'd be honored to share another tale with you and your cabinet... Let the record reflect that this is a true story...

"Every morning, Brittany Geldert stepped off the bus and bolted through the double doors of Fred Moore Middle School, her nerves already on high alert, bracing for the inevitable: "DYKE."

"Pretending not to hear, Brittany would walk briskly to her locker, past the sixth, seventh and eighth graders who loitered in menacing packs. "WHORE."

"Like many thirteen-year-olds, Brittany knew seventh grade was a living hell. But what she didn't know was that she was caught in the crossfire of a culture war being waged by local evangelicals, inspired by their high-profile congressional representative Nolan Barnes who graduated from Anoka High School and, until recently, was a member of one of the most conservative churches in the area. When Christian activists who considered gays an abomination forced a measure through the school board forbidding the discussion of homosexuality in the district's public schools, kids like Brittany were unknowingly thrust into the heart of a clash that was about to become intertwined with tragedy.

"Brittany didn't look like most girls in blue-collar Anoka, Minnesota. Brittany was a low-voiced, stocky girl who dressed in baggy jeans and her dad's Marine Corps sweatshirt. By age thirteen, she'd been taunted as a cunt long before such a word had made much sense...

"When she told administrators about the abuse they were strangely unresponsive, even though bullying was a subject often discussed in school board meetings. The district maintained a comprehensive five-page anti-bullying policy and held diversity trainings on racial and gender sensitivity. Yet, when it came to Brittany's harassment, school officials usually told her to ignore it, always glossing over the sexually charged insults. Like the time Brittany had complained about being called a "FAT DYKE": the school's pompous principal, looking pained, had suggested Brittany prepare herself for the next round of teasing with snappy comebacks – "I can lose the weight, but you're stuck with your ugly face" – never acknowledging that she had been called a "DYKE," as though that part was OK. As though the fact that Brittany was bisexual made her fair game."

CHAPTER TWENTY-SIX— HIS AND HIS WEDDING RINGS...

"So maybe she was a fat dyke, Brittany thought morosely. Maybe she deserved the teasing. She would have been shocked to know the truth behind the adults' inaction: no one would come to her aid for fear of violating the district-wide policy requiring school personnel to stay "NEUTRAL" on issues of homosexuality. All Brittany knew was that she was on her own, vulnerable and ashamed, and needed to find her best friend Samantha fast.

"Like Brittany, eighth grader Samantha Johnson was a husky tomboy too, outgoing with a big smile and a silly streak to match Brittany's own. Sam was also bullied for her look – short hair, dark clothing, and lack of girly affect – but she merrily shrugged off the abuse. When Sam's volleyball teammates' taunting got rough – barring her from the girls' locker room, yelling "you're a guy!" – she simply stopped going to practice. After school, Sam would encourage Brittany to join her in privately mocking their tormentors, and the girls would parade around Brittany's house speaking in valley girl squeals, wearing bras over their shirts, collapsing in laughter. They'd become as close as sisters in the year since Sam had moved from North Dakota following her parents' divorce, and Sam had quickly become Brittany's beacon. Sam was even helping to start a GAY-STRAIGHT Alliance club, as a safe haven for misfits like them, though the club's progress was stalled by the school district that, among other things, was queasy about the club's flagrant use of the word "GAY."

"Religious conservatives have called GSAs "sex clubs," and sure enough, the local religious right loudly objected to them. "This is an assault on moral standards," read one recent letter to the community paper. "Let's stop this dangerous nonsense before it's too late and more young boys and girls are encouraged to "come out" and practice their "gayness" right in their own school's homosexual club."

"Brittany admired Sam's courage and tried to emulate her insouciance and stoicism. So Brittany was bewildered when one day in November 2009, on the school bus home, a sixth grade boy slid in next to her and asked quaveringly, "Did you hear Sam said she's going to kill herself?"

"Brittany considered the question. No way. How many times had she seen Sam roll her eyes and announce, "Ugh, I'm gonna kill myself" over some insignificant thing?

""Don't worry, you'll see Sam tomorrow," Brittany reassured her friend as they got off the bus. But as she trudged toward her house, she couldn't stop turning it over in her mind. A boy in the district had already committed suicide just days into the school year – TJ Hayes, a sixteen-year-old at Blaine High School – so she knew such things were possible. But Sam Johnson?

"Brittany tried to keep the thought at bay. Finally, she confided in her mother. "This isn't something to kid about, Brittany," her mom scolded, snatching the kitchen cordless phone and taking it down the hall to call the Johnsons. A minute later she returned, her face a mask of shock and terror. "Honey, I'm so sorry. We're too late," she said tonelessly as Brittany's knees buckled: thirteen-year-old Sam had climbed into the bathtub after school and shot herself in the mouth with her own hunting rifle. No one at school had seen her suicide coming. No one saw the rest of them coming either...

"Sam's death lit the fuse of a suicide epidemic that would take the lives of nine local students in under two years, a rate so high that child psychologist Dan Austin, Executive Director of the Minnesota-based Suicide Awareness Voices of Education, declared the Anoka-Hennepin School District the site of a "suicide cluster," adding that the crisis might hold an element of contagion: suicidal thoughts had become catchy, like a lethal virus. "Here you had a large number of suicides that are really closely connected, all within one school district, in a small amount of time. Kids started to feel that the normal response to stress was to take your life."

"Brittany couldn't stop thinking about Sam, a reel that looped endlessly in her head: Sam dancing to one of their favorite metal bands, Drowning Pool. Sam was dead in the tub with the back of her head blown off. Sam's ashes were in an urn, her coffin empty at her wake.

"She couldn't sleep. Her grades fell. Her daily harassment at school continued but now, she was without her best friend to help her cope. At home Brittany played the good daughter, cleaning the house and performing her brother's chores unasked, all in a valiant attempt to maintain some family peace after the bank took their house and both parents lost their jobs in quick succession. Then Brittany started cutting herself. Just eleven days after Sam's death, on November 22, 2009 came yet another suicide: a Blaine High School student – fifteen-year-old Aaron Jurek – the district's third suicide in just three months. After Christmas break, an Andover High School senior, Nick Lockwood, became the district's fourth casualty: a boy who had never publicly identified as gay, but had nonetheless been teased as such. Suicide number five followed, that of recent Blaine High School grad Kevin Buchman, who had no apparent LGBT connection...

"Before the end of the school year there would be a sixth suicide, fifteen-year-old July Barrick of Champlin Park High School, who was also bullied for being perceived as gay and who'd complained to her mother that classmates had started an "I hate July Barrick" Facebook page. As mental health counselors were hurriedly dispatched to each affected school, the district was blanketed by a sense of mourning and frightened shock. "It has taken a collective toll," says Northdale Middle School psychologist Colleen Casey. "Everyone has just been reeling – students, teachers. There's been just such a profound sadness."

"In the wake of Sam's suicide, Brittany couldn't seem to stop crying. She'd disappear for hours with her cellphone turned off, taking long walks by Elk Creek or hiding in a nearby cemetery. "Promise me you won't take your life," her father begged. "Promise you'll come to me before anything."

"Brittany couldn't promise. In March 2010, she was hospitalized for a week."

"Whatever happened to the lad Justin?" asked President Dotson as tears cascaded down his cheeks.

"In April, Justin came home from school and found his mother at the top of the stairs, tending to the saltwater fish tank. "MOM," he said tentatively, "a kid told me at school today that I'm gonna go to hell because I'm gay."

""That's not true. God loves everybody," his mom replied. "That kid needs to go home and read his Bible."

"Justin shrugged and smiled, then retreated to his room. It had been a hard day: the annual "Day of Truth" had been held at school, an evangelical event then sponsored by the ANTI-GAY ministry Exodus International, whose mission is to usher gays back to wholeness and "victory in Christ" by converting them to HETEROSEXUALITY. Day of Truth has been a font of controversy that has bounced in and out of the courts. Its legality was affirmed last March, when a Federal Appeals court ruled that two Naperville, Illinois high school students' Day of Truth t-shirts reading BE HAPPY, NOT GAY were protected by their First Amendment rights (however, the event, now sponsored by Focus on the Family, has been renamed "DAY OF DIALOGUE")...

"Local churches had been touting the program, and students had obediently shown up at Anoka High School wearing Day of Truth t-shirts, preaching in the halls about the sin of homosexuality. Justin wanted to brush them off, but was troubled by their proselytizing. Secretly, he had begun to worry that maybe he was an abomination, like the Bible said.

"Justin was trying not to care what anyone else thought and to be true to himself. He surrounded himself with a bevy of girlfriends who cherished him for his sweet, sunny disposition. He played cello in the orchestra, practicing for hours up in his room, where he'd covered one wall with mementos of good times: taped-up movie ticket stubs, photos, Christmas cards, etc., etc... Justin had even briefly dated a boy, a seventeen-year-old he'd met online who attended a nearby high school. The relationship didn't end well: the boyfriend had cheated on him, and compounding Justin's hurt, his coming out had earned Justin HATEFUL Facebook messages from other teens – some from those he didn't even know – telling him he was a fag who didn't deserve to live. At least his freshman year of high school was nearly over. He thought to himself, only three more years to go. He wondered how he would ever make it.

""Justin?" Tammy Aaberg rapped on her son's locked bedroom door again. It was past noon and not a peep from inside, unusual for Justin.

""Justin?" She could hear her own voice rising as she pounded harder, suddenly overtaken by a wild terror she couldn't name. "Justin!" she yelled. Tammy grabbed a screwdriver and loosened the doorknob. She pushed open the door.

"He was wearing his Anoka High School sweatpants and an old soccer shirt. His feet were dangling off the ground. Justin was hanging from the frame of his futon, which he'd taken out from under his mattress and stood upright in the corner of his room. Screaming, Tammy ran to hold him and recoiled at the touch of his cold skin. His limp body was grotesquely bloated – her baby – eyes closed, head lolling to the right, a dried smear of saliva trailing from the corner of his mouth. His cheeks were strafed with scratch marks, as though in his final moments he'd tried to claw his noose loose. He'd cinched the woven belt so tightly that the mortician would have a hard time masking the imprint that it left in the flesh above Justin's collar.

"Still screaming, Tammy ran to call 911. She didn't notice the cellphone on the floor below Justin's feet containing his last words, a text in the wee hours: :-(he had typed to a friend."

CHAPTER TWENTY-SEVEN— SAME-SEX LOVEMAKING...

"Though some members of the Anoka-Hennepin School Board had been appalled by "NO HOMO PROMO" since its passage fourteen years earlier, it wasn't until 2009 that the board brought the policy up for review, after a student named Alex Merritt filed a complaint with the State Department of Human Rights, claiming he'd been gay-bashed by two of his teachers during high school. According to the complaint, the teachers had announced in front of students that Merritt, who is straight, "swings both ways," speculated that he wore women's clothing, and compared him to a Wisconsin man who had sex with a dead deer. The teachers denied the charges, but the school district paid twenty-five thousand dollars to settle the complaint. Soon, representatives from the gay rights group OutFront Minnesota began making inquiries at board meetings. "NO HOMO PROMO" was starting to look like a risky policy.

"It was clear that it might risk a lawsuit. But while board members agreed that such an overtly anti-gay policy needed to be scrapped, they also agreed that some guidelines were needed to not only help teachers navigate a topic as inflammatory as homosexuality, but to appease the area's evangelical activists. So the legal department wrote a broad new course of action with language intended to give a respectful nod to the topic – but also an equal measure of respect to the ANTI-GAY contingent. The new policy was circulated to staff without a word of introduction. (Parents were not alerted at all, unless they happened to be diligent online readers of board meeting minutes). And while "NO HOMO PROMO" had at least been clear, the new sexual orientation curriculum policy mostly just puzzled the teachers who would be responsible for enforcing it.

"It read: "Anoka-Hennepin staff, in the course of their professional duties, shall remain neutral on matters regarding sexual orientation including but not limited to student-led discussions." It quickly became known as the "NEUTRALITY" policy. No one could figure out what it meant."

"What is neutral?" asked Catilina as she diverted her attention to the Derringer.

"Hey, don't interrupt my boyfriend while he's giving you a synopsis on the fickle "NO HOMO PROMO" policy."

"Pardon me... Please continue," stated Catilina as she removed the Ruger from her shoulder holster.

"As I was saying, English teachers worried they'd get in trouble for teaching books by GAY authors or books with gay characters. Social studies teachers wondered what to do if a student wrote a term paper on gay rights, or how to address current events like "DON'T ASK, DON'T TELL." Health teachers were faced with the impossible task of teaching about AIDS awareness and SAFE SEX without mentioning homosexuality. Many teachers decided, once again, to keep gay issues form the curriculum altogether rather than chance saying something that could be interpreted as anything other than neutral."

"There has been widespread confusion," stated Catilina while covertly adjusting the safety latch on the Ruger. "You ask five people how to interpret the policy and you get five different answers."

"Silenced by fear, gay teachers have become more vigilant than ever to avoid mention of their personal lives. And in closeting themselves, they inadvertently ensured that many students had NO REAL-LIFE GAY ROLE MODELS."

"I was told by teachers that it's not safe to come out," shouted the gay chap clutching the Derringer. "I felt like I couldn't have a picture of my boyfriend in my school locker. When teacher Jefferson Fietek was outed in the community paper, which referred to him as an "OPEN HOMOSEXUAL," he didn't feel he could address the situation with his students, even as they passed the newspaper around, tittering. When one finally asked, "Are you gay?" he panicked. He was terrified to answer that question.

"The silence of adults was deafening. At my old high school, I would hear people calling people "FAGS" all the time, without being addressed. Teachers just didn't respond. At Andover High School, when three kids calling him a "faggot pushed tenth grader Sam Pinilla to the ground" he saw a teacher nearby who did nothing to stop the assault. At Anoka High School, a tenth grade girl became so upset at being mocked as a "LESBO" and a "SINNER" – within earshot of teachers – that she complained to an assistant principal, who counseled her to "lay low." The girl would later attempt suicide. At Anoka Middle School for the Arts, after Kyle Rooker was urinated on from above in a boys' bathroom stall, an assistant principal told him, "IT WAS PROBABLY WATER."

Jackson Middle School seventh grader Dylon Frei was passed notes saying, "Get out of this town, FAG." When a teacher intercepted one such note, she simply threw it away.

"The following year, after Dylon was hit in the head with a binder and called "FAG," the assistant principal told Dylon that since there was no proof of the incident, she could take no action. By contrast, Dylon and others saw how the same teachers who ignored ANTI-GAY INSULTS were quick to reprimand kids who uttered racial slurs. It further reinforced the message resonating throughout the district: GAY KIDS SIMPLY DIDN'T DESERVE PROTECTION."

"You know what... I've heard about enough," shouted Catilina. "I have no sympathy for these gay teens. Thirteen-year-old girls and fourteen-year-old boys have no right to flaunt their sexual preference, no right to prance around school grounds professing and promoting homosexuality. I vividly recall the first time I observed two fourteen-year-old boys French kissing. I almost puked... A part of me wanted to remove their tongues and feed them to a famished seagull."

"If Carla ever heard you make a flagrant statement like that, she'd have you drowned in boiling-hot sewage matter," shouted the gay lad clutching the Derringer.

"FYI lover boy, I've had the luxury of ridiculing Mr. KARL SIMS when he first slithered out of the closet and informed his peers that he was attracted to men. I fucked his first boyfriend and stole his first car. The evolution and drag queen-driven transformation of Karl Sims is comical and despicable. The proverbial "empire" he's constructed and the infinite wealth he's slyly obtained is indeed miraculous. The full sex change he's in pursuit of won't fill the void in his life, nor will it validate his shitty existence. The cosmetic surgery he had done recently will in no way grant him the soft ladylike facial features that he craves. The provisions that he perpetually sends to cursed third world countries won't secure him a chateau in heaven, nor will he be remembered for his selfless deeds. In the eyes of many corrupt confederates, rogue Republicans and dogmatic Democrats, Karl will always be a voguish villain whose aspiration in life is to become a virtuous vixen that'll be feared and revered like the wife of President Nixon."

"It's blasphemous to say cruel things about a QUINTESSENTIAL QUEEN," shouted the chap in possession of the Derringer.

"He's no queen," shouted Catilina while glaring at the gay couple, "he's a crownless king that conducts himself like a quick-tempered queen that's allergic to warm pussy and cold beer."

"You watch your mouth, young lady," shouted the fellow holding the Derringer. "Carla's a pillar of the gay community. The last SKANK that spoke slanderously about Carla in front of us was tackled, shackled and towed to The Pink House."

"You two queers couldn't tackle and shackle a lost lamb," stated Catilina as she got to her feet. "If I had another sixty seconds to squander, I'd have you two lovebirds relinquish your personal effects. I'd force you to swallow that Derringer, and as for you... I'd make you spit-shine these glass slippers I'm wearing."

"BON VOYAGE, BITCH," shouted one of the men as Catilina sashayed over to her awaiting fawn-colored Ferrari.

Before climbing into the topless Ferrari, Catilina re-holstered her weapon and placed her laptop on the rear seat.

"Since when do you fraternize with homosexuals?" asked Catilina's boy toy as she sat in the passenger seat.

"I wasn't fraternizing with those fags, I was simply conveying to them that FAGGOTS are like spoiled milk and pestilent parasites that need to be round up like cattle and diplomatically deported to Mars..."

"Don't say things like that, babe," stated her boy toy as he swerved into traffic. "You're too stunning to make comments like that. You have to somehow learn to soften your heart toward gay people. Ninety percent of all gay people are selfless, creative and innovative. Every homosexual I've met is utterly solution-oriented and family-oriented. They're interesting entities – many are soft-spoken and outspoken. Unbeknownst to the potbellied pricks in the White House, the gay men and women that reside in America are becoming the pioneers of the twenty-first century, the trendsetters and trailblazers of this era... They've created their very own genre. They're superbly influential. Many have found their niche and found a way to become one with the new money, align themselves with those that come from old money, and upstage the humanitarians of the past without trying."

"They're swine, babe," mumbled Catilina. "One must never exalt swine, nor cast their pearls before swine."

"Your perception of homosexuals is beyond jaded," stated the boy toy as the scowl on his face took shape. "Homosexuals are more charitable than the creeps in Congress. Gay men seem to have hearts the size of small planets. Lesbians are more liberal than the lecherous lawmakers that dwell in gated communities. Transgendered people are always trying to facilitate and promote the uplift of fallen humanity... Transsexuals are always making a sincere effort to increase the wellbeing of mankind, as by charitable donations. Openly gay couples have a love for mankind in general. They're awesome people. I find it very unattractive that my girlfriend has a tarnished perception of same-sex couples."

"Pull the car over," shouted Catilina. "Pull the car over now."

"I'm not your girlfriend," stated Catilina as he pulled the Ferrari over and parked behind a silver Volvo. "I've never called myself your girlfriend. It's dishonorable and disgusting that you have such a twisted impulse to always vocalize your adoration for gay people. You remind me of this gay advocate I once dated. He, too, would go on and on about the accolades and grand accomplishments of LGBT members. I'm an entity; therefore I'm entitled to my personal opinion of homosexuality. I view boys that are attracted to other boys as amorous psychopaths.

"A man that finds nothing appealing and nothing extraordinary about a pulsating pussy is clearly psychotic. Girls that desire to be sexually intimate with other girls are sassy sociopaths. Any bitch that doesn't LOVE the taste of warm semen and the phenomenal feeling of a ten-inch penis being skillfully rammed repeatedly inside of her is a bitch that the gods frown upon."

"You're a witless witch," shouted Catilina's boy toy. "A cunt like you should be stoned for being so biased and narrow-minded."

"Did you just call me a cunt?" asked Catilina as she swiftly extracted the Ruger from its holster. "I'm a cunt, huh? Define cunt... Better yet, when you're being airlifted to the trauma unit, be sure to candidly explain to the EMTs and investigators that a cunt by the name of Catilina Ortega is solely responsible for these lumps and lacerations..."

Just as the boy toy was attempting to make sense of Catilina's ominous remark, he was struck in the mouth with the hilt of the firearm. Upon impact, one of his left teeth was chipped and both of his incisors were dislodged from their sockets. As his two front teeth greeted his tonsils, Catilina delivered another blow to his mouth. The second blow to his mouth cracked four of his bottom teeth and administered a hairline fracture to his jaw. Blood and shards of teeth choked him after the third blow landed. The third wallop struck his pinky finger as he made a strategic attempt to shield his mouth from being awarded another blow. Pedestrians and several motorists gawked in disbelief as Catilina repeatedly struck her companion with the butt of the Ruger. After devilishly delivering the thirteenth blow to his face, she opened the driver's-side door and kicked him onto the roadway. The gash above his right eye and the gash across the bridge of his nose leaked blood profusely. The few abrasions in the center of his forehead were relatively minor compared to the gash in his upper lip. As Catilina climbed into the driver's seat, she was pleased to discover that the attack left her lover unconscious and in need of facial restoration.

"Good riddance, handsome," shouted Catilina as she slammed the gearshift into fourth and glided into traffic. The blood that covered her fingers and soiled her blouse repulsed her.

On her lap sat the bloody Ruger. The splattered blood that peppered her face and hair began to dry as she nonchalantly zipped through traffic. While driving, Catilina assessed the amount of blood

Abdul Robinson

that sullied the inner driver's-side door panel, tarnished the sleek steering wheel and blotched the driver's seat...

CHAPTER TWENTY-EIGHT— SAME-SEX SPARTANS

After nonchalantly choking out one of the gossipy damsels, I stood in front of the vanity mirror and adjusted my wig. Pleased with my overall appearance I exited the powder room, hoping to encounter the other two backbiting broads that had left their friend to fend for herself...

While making a beeline to the gymnasium, I erased the scowl from my face and replaced it with a delighted smile. Seconds later I entered the gymnasium and my peace was abruptly restored as two dozen or so cheerful orphans raced over to me, with snack fare in one hand and lollipops in their other. While rationing out fatherly hugs and motherly kisses to the precious orphans, I peered over at Loyd and informed him that I had to manhandle a biased bitch while in the ladies room...

"Are you fucking kidding me?" mumbled Loyd as I planted a dry kiss on the forehead of a fatherless boy.

"Watch your language in front of these kids," I authoritatively whispered after administering a bear hug to a motherless young girl that was cramming a fistful of five-dollar bills into her Dora lunchbox.

"Let's go," stated Loyd as he grabbed me by my arm and led me out of the gymnasium.

"Let go of me, before I shatter your wrist in front of these children," I jokingly stated as I submissively allowed my man to usher me off the premises.

"Babe, for the thousandth time, you can't physically injure every person you encounter that shuns homosexuality. You're gonna end up in prison."

"The thought of ending up in prison will never deter me from reprimanding those that verbally express their disenchantment with same-sex courting, and I sure as hell will never allow the thought of going to prison prevent me from distributing grueling punishment to those that display contempt for the openly gay... A damsel of my caliber would surely excel and effortlessly thrive in a penal institution."

"What the hell happened in the lavatory?" asked Loyd as he hailed a taxicab via sharp whistle.

"Three biased bimbos were having an inappropriate discussion about same-sex nuptials. One of them made a comment about wanting to sleep with you. Then they started saying cruel things about my wig and my attire. They were chatty and catty, babe."

"That still doesn't give you the right to engage in combat," stated Loyd as the cab stopped in front of us.

"What's a lady to do?" I sternly asked as my man and I climbed into the rear of the taxi. "They were being inconsiderate and slanderous. Therefore, I responded accordingly."

"Where to?" asked the cabdriver as he adjusted the dial on the mile-tallying apparatus.

"The Willis Tower," stated Loyd as he rested his head on my right shoulder.

"You should be proud of me, honey. I actually allowed two of the three women to elude my wrath as I allotted a small portion of divine retribution to one young lady that flaunted her disapproval of same-sex dating. I wasted no time putting the thoughtless SKANK in the sleeper..."

"Please don't tell me you choked the young lady out," stated Loyd as I toyed with the police shield emblem that was affixed to his leather belt.

"Of course I choked her out. She's utterly lucky that I didn't crack her windpipe and force her to guzzle toilet water. The last skank that made vilifying remarks about people that indulge in homosexuality, I personally hacked off all ten of her toes and later forced her to chew and swallow them."

"Will you guys be attending the candlelight vigil in Minneapolis for the victims of gay bullying?" asked the Iranian cabby as he made a left turn on Michigan Avenue.

"Isn't that vigil being held this weekend?" asked Loyd as he ran his fingers through my hair.

"I'm not sure, Sir," stated the cabdriver. "I've got a poster that discloses the details about the candlelight vigil. Would you two like to assess the flyer?"

"Yes, we would," stated Loyd as the cabby extracted the poster from the glove compartment.

As he handed me the flyer, it dawned on me that this poster was an ANTI-SUICIDE memorial poster. At the heading of the poster was the memorial phrase: "Gone too soon." Printed on the poster were TEN thumbnail photographs of dashing teenagers, six boys and four girls. Directly underneath each photo was the person's date of birth and the person's date of death. Directly above each photograph was the person's legal name. In the lower left-hand corner was a photo of a teenage girl named Emily Nicole Trotter, date of birth 9/23/92, date of departure 9/13/09. Above the photo of Emily was a pic of Samantha Johnson, born 7/7/96, died 11/11/09. To the left was a photo of Cole Wilson and Justin Aaberg, date of birth for Justin 3/9/95, date of death 7/9/10.

"Babe, these are actual photographs of the teens that killed themselves in Minneapolis."

"Are those the teens that attended Anoka High School and Fred Moore Middle School?" asked Loyd as he gazed at the poster.

"It doesn't disclose their school but I'm sure I know what school this lad by the name of Thomas John Hayes was enrolled in."

"He's stunning," mumbled Loyd as he gazed at the photo of T.J. Hayes.

"This here is July Barrick and this here is Aaron Jurek. I'd like to disembowel the jerkoffs that bullied these teens and I'd like to hang the schoolteachers that allowed these teens to be bullied by their entitled peers."

"Look at this handsome Jordan Yenor and the regal Kevin Buchman," stated Loyd as he ran his index finger across the two photos.

"Kylie Cowan has a beautiful smile, doesn't she?" asked the cabby as he parked in front of the Willis Tower.

"What's the damage, Sir?" asked Loyd as he disunited three twenty-dollar bills from the wad of bills that were crammed into his wallet.

"That'll be $38.88. And feel free to keep the flyer."

"Here's sixty bucks. Keep the change. And keep the motor running," shouted Loyd as we climbed out of the taxicab.

CHAPTER TWENTY-NINE— GAY PRIDE

"Where there's gay marriage comes... the rise of gay divorce," shouted Marvin as he scribbled anti-gay insignia onto his picket sign. "The other night while in Boys Town I encountered a stud wearing a Roberto Cavalli amoeba-print viscose jersey dress."

"Did he try to hit on you?" asked a young lady as she took a selfie while clutching her own picket sign.

"Of course he tried to hit on me. Gay men are always trying to seduce me. This creep had the effrontery to invite me to Tracee Ellis Ross's birthday party in the Hamptons."

"Please tell me you lovingly declined," shouted the young lady as she took another selfie.

"You're damn right I declined. Do I strike you as the kind of chap that'll be interested in attending an all-pink party in the Hamptons????"

"I wouldn't be caught dead at a soiree surrounded by people whose top aspiration in life is to someday marry someone of the same gender. I was a tad intrigued when the stud in the dress mentioned that RuPaul, Ian McKellan, Perez Hilton, Neil Patrick Harris and Raven Simone would all be attending the all-pink party..."

"You should've accepted the invite," shouted his other colleague, who was preparing his own anti-gay picket sign.

"I'm sure there's going to be a slew of straight men at the slumber party. An all-pink party in the Hamptons will surely be epic and tasteful, but I had to decline. I've got a reputation that I must protect at all costs. The last thing I need is for photos of me mingling with openly gay dudes to be uploaded on the Internet. Social media has the egregious ability of tarnishing a person's brand..."

"There's no fucking way I would've turned down an invite to attend an all-pink party in the Hamptons. As much as I despise fags, I would have attended that same-sex Soirée and accomplished some monumental networking."

"When I think of an LGBT pink party in the Hamptons, I think of Portia De Rossi, Anne Heche, George Takei, Kristanna Loken from *Terminator 3*, Jim Parsons, Neil Patrick Harris and Jim Nabors."

"Well, FYI, when I think about a same-sex soiree being held in the Hamptons, I think of upscale entities like Rob Halford, George Michael, Elton John, Little Richard, Boy George and Queen Latifah..."

"A party in the Hamptons doesn't appeal to my party boy nature, especially when one is certain that the entire gay community will be present, including Rosie O'Donnell, Paul Reubens, Wanda Sykes, Michael Sam, Clay Aiken, Lady Gaga, Eddie Long, and Jason Collins. The belle of the ball will be someone influential and dauntless like Don Lemon or Anderson Cooper."

"I wonder if the actress that played Hilary on the hit show Fresh Prince of Bel-Air will be at the bash,"

"Karyn Parsons? She'll be there. She supports anything that's smothered in homosexuality."

"The man in the Cavalli dress did state that David Burtka, Sam Smith, and Michael Arceneaux would be attending the party."

"How's your sign coming along?" asked the dame that took another selfie while clutching her picket sign.

"It's coming along fine. I just find it odd that your dad and his political playmates are going to pay us several grand to manufacture three hundred anti-gay picket signs and participate in a pep rally that opposes dudes dating dudes and damsels courting dames."

"My dad's a lobbyist and so are his pals. They don't respect the laws of individuality, nor do they grasp the rational concept of EQUALITY. It's been indoctrinated in them to reject, discard and discredit those that are sexually active with members of the same sex."

"Your dad does a grand job of concealing his hate toward

homosexuality and the advocacy of same-sex parenting. Does your mom share similar views as your dad in matters pertaining to boys having boyfriends and women being salaciously intimate with other females?"

"My mom's a stoic poet. For the most part, she often displays a snobbish level of neutrality in public because many of her Instagram followers are gay socialites, but behind closed doors she spends hours watching soft core girl-on-girl porn."

"My mom isn't a fan of girl-on-girl porn... but she goes have a schoolgirl crush on Carla Sims."

"Isn't Carla that prissy broad that's always gallivanting around town in that tricked-out Rolls Royce?"

"Yep, that's her. She's a diva, an official five-star chick. Her shoe game is fierce and bananas."

"Isn't she a gay advocate?"

"She's a transgendered hussy," shouted Tony's father as he swaggered into the garage, clutching a picket sign that had the phrase "BAN GAY Marriage" printed on the placard. "A transgendered hussy that's attempting to revivify a same-sex revolt. She's spoiled milk, a cowboy that doesn't mind peep toe pumps and sheer garter belts."

"You shouldn't judge her, Dad," shouted Tony as he avoided eye contact with his judgmental father. "She has a God-given right to cross-dress and sleep with whom she pleases. Every other week you pay me and my friends to construct these picket signs so you and your buddies can march downtown wielding these inflammatory placards. Do you have any clue what'll happen to you and your associates if the Defenders of Same-Sex Courtship receive intel that you all are downtown brandishing picket signs that loathe gay marriage? You all will most likely be rounded up like livestock and force-fed each other's feces."

"To hell with the bloody Defenders of Same-Sex Courtship,"

shouted Tony's dad as he raised his picket sign over his head. "The Defenders of Same-Sex Courtship are a bunch of dudes aspiring to become damsels, and a bunch of dames aspiring to become dudes. It's flat-out iniquitous to see lads romantically pursuing chaps, and it's absurd that debutantes and damsels are trying to wed other ladies. It's verboten to allow gay men to adopt children and introduce them to the LGBT way of life. It's illicit and taboo for two females to construct a makeshift family and exchange vows."

"You shouldn't say things like that, Dad," shouted Tony as he flung one of the picket signs up against the lawnmower that sat in the corner. "You make these mean-spirited statements, yet I've seen you being chummy with Roger and Martin and they're both openly gay."

"Let the record reflect, son, that I fraternize with Martin because he helps me pay our mortgage every month, and as for Roger, I associate with him in a congenial way because he provided me with the revenue and the avenue that helped my mother, your grandmother, open up her very own coffee café."

"Granny's a hypocritical woman," shouted Tony while making eye contact with his father. "She claims to not be fond of homosexuals, yet she strategically opened her coffeehouse directly across the street from LGBT HEADQUARTERS. Ninety percent of her coffee clientele are openly gay men and women. I've seen her smile in their faces as she fills their orders and snarl behind their backs. She's a hypocrite and that alone is why I seldom visit her coffee shop."

"My mother's a good woman," stated Tony's dad as he glared at his son.

"She's not a good woman," shouted Tony. "I've witnessed her gulping down Irish whiskey and confiding in her six cats about one day retrieving her sniper rifle from the attic and slaughtering a colony of same-sex newlyweds."

"She's harmless," shouted Tony's dad.

"Harmless my ass," yelled Tony. "I've seen the way she dismantles and reassembles that rifle of hers. If I were you, I'd have her relinquish that rifle before she does something foul, flagrant and treasonous."

"I've paid you and your pill-purchasing pals to construct anti-gay picket signs, not to brief me on my mother's shortcomings. Get back to work. The homophobia march is in two days. I expect these signs to be done by tomorrow afternoon."

"What inspired you and your handpicked cronies to host and choreograph a homophobic rally?" asked Tony.

"You're a kid, son, you haven't licked enough pussy, squandered enough cash and drunk enough beers yet to properly process why we Democrats and Republicans do what we do. And if I took the time to explain to you in layman's terms what it is that inspires me to orchestrate these monthly anti-gay demonstrations, you and your teammates wouldn't be able to appraise or appreciate the variety of things that inspire me to stage anti-equality rallies. Now my question to you is: why the fuck don't you have a girlfriend yet? Does the sacred scent of pussy and perfume annoy you and your gothic comrades? Does the thought of sneaking teenage girls into your room ever cross your mind? I personally purchased you a sports car that attracts females, yet for some odd reason you don't use the chariot to fleece the cute cheerleaders from the jocks that bullied you and your friends in middle school... When I was your age, I was an astute skirt-chaser, a radical rake that chased fast money and fast women. I didn't spend my evenings in my dad's basement as you do, playing the XBOX with shirtless boys that wear eyeliner and snug-fitting trousers. And what's this I hear about you entertaining the thought of getting your lip pierced and your eyebrows arched?"

"Quit being dramatic, Dad... You're embarrassing me in front of my friends. As for the notion of getting my lip pierced, it's something that I think will be badass. And everyone knows that I've been allowing Marcus to arch my eyebrows since the sixth grade."

"Who the hell is Marcus?"

"He's a boy that's valiant and gallant," shouted Tony's best friend Billy as he applied glue and glitter to one of the picket signs.

"He's dreamy," stated Sierra as she took another selfie.

"What's going on with you, son? Are you attracted to boys?"

"No... I'm not attracted to chaps. But boys are indeed attracted to me. When I go to the mall, guys hit on me all the time. It's difficult not to blush and value the male attention. Oh... and just so you know, the rancid odor and vile taste of teenage pussy is something that doesn't sexually arouse me or my Instagram followers."

"I'm smitten with the aromatic scent that dwells within the inner confines of a woman's vaginal cavity," Sierra chimed in as she placed her phone in the back pocket of her loose-fitting cargo shorts.

"I've sampled several palpitating pussies, Mr. Drysdale," shouted Billy, "and I wasn't flabbergasted or enchanted by the fact that each dame rudely squirted cum into my mouth."

"Are you gay, Billy?" asked Mr. Drysdale as he gawked at the open-toed sandals Billy had on.

"No... I'm not gay," shouted Billy, "but I have kissed quite a few boys during spring break at band camp."

"What about you, Tony? Have you ever kissed any boys while away at band camp?" asked Mr. Drysdale as he glared at Billy.

"Nope," mumbled Tony as he blushed uncontrollably.

"You like boys, huh?" asked Mr. Drysdale as he shoved Tony up against the tool cabinet. "I oughta take one of these signs and crack you upside of your skull..."

"If you shove him again, I'll personally remove your kidneys and covertly feed them to my Aunt Jessica's two bullmastiffs," shouted Sierra as she removed a sinister-looking bolo from her L.L. Bean gym bag...

CHAPTER THIRTY— SAME-SEX UNION

"Hi, handsome," shouted Mrs. Drysdale as Loyd entered the coffeehouse that was located across the street from The Pink House.

"Good evening, ma'am," replied Detective Stevenson as he sat on the swivel-stool.

"Where's that charming partner of yours?" asked Mrs. Drysdale as she placed a complimentary slice of cheesecake in front of a patron that was seated on the swivel-stool to the right of Loyd.

"He's off duty today. Yesterday was his Friday," stated Loyd as a fellow wearing a lotus-colored leotard, some Merona moccasins and a tutu strolled into the coffee shop. The leggings he had on were turnip-colored and so was the fedora that was perched and tilted atop his dirty blond wig.

"Bah humbug," mumbled Mrs. Drysdale as the transgendered patron sat on the stool to the left of Loyd. "Hi sweetie," shouted Mrs. Drysdale, hoping that Loyd didn't detect her detestation for the openly gay patron.

"Who's the hunk?" asked the fellow wearing the ballet skirt as he batted his eyes and bit down on his bottom lip.

"He's a narc," shouted the lesbian that was given the complimentary slice of cheesecake.

"A narc that's cute as a button... You got a name, narc?" asked the dude in the leotard.

"My name is Loyd."

"I bet the women at the precinct appreciate your presence," stated

Mrs. Drysdale as she placed a cup of joe in front of the cheesecake recipient.

"What brings you to this LGBT watering hole?" asked the lad in the tutu.

"My significant other is always giving rave reviews about the raspberry cobbler and caffeinated beverages that you personally prepare," stated Loyd as Sebastian swaggered into the coffeehouse, holding hands with a young man that had a feminine walk and a boyish smile.

"My boo and I would like two espressos to go," shouted Sebastian as he waved at the chap in the ballet shirt.

"Two espressos, coming right up," replied Mrs. Drysdale.

"I'd like an iced latte," shouted the lesbian.

"I'd like a cup of cappuccino," stated Loyd, "and a sample of that raspberry cobbler."

"Hi Sebastian," the young man in the leotard chimed in. "Have you heard about Tyler Clementi?"

"Yes... When I first heard the story of Tyler Clementi my heart broke. This young Rutgers University student with so much to live for jumped to his death from New York's George Washington Bridge because he felt so humiliated and betrayed by his roommates secretly taping him in a sexual encounter with another man. This afternoon I asked myself, had Clementi been heterosexual, would anyone have put him out there like that? And what would have happened to me if anyone had found out about my secret when I was in the Air Force..."

"When did you actually come out of the closet?" asked Loyd as Mrs. Drysdale placed the small bowl of cobbler and the cup of cappuccino in front of him.

"In 2008 I was living in Utah and had just broken up with my first boyfriend. My father called and wondered why I sounded so depressed. I finally confessed to him that I was GAY and that I was heartbroken about my relationship ending. At first he very calmly said, "I love you. I don't care what you are because you are a noble person." Then several months later he started asking, "Don't you want children? What about your career?" He thought that I could change. He thought that he could pray the gay away.

"It befuddled the fuck out of me that he didn't understand that I couldn't just make myself become something I'm not. After my brother and sister died, he realized what was important in life and finally accepted it. I'm speaking for the Tyler Clementis of the world: if your son or daughter tells you that he or she is gay, assure them that you love them no matter what. Be mindful of the environment that you create around them because they learn from you firsthand and transfer those attitudes into the world."

"Heterosexuals in general have a very limited definition of masculinity," shouted Loyd after sampling the raspberry cobbler. "I make it my business to shun bigotry and discrimination. I'm not going to lie – there's a definite stigma in the black community that being gay is the worst thing possible."

"Let me say that not all gay men are feminine," shouted the man in the ballet skirt.

"Sharing my story hasn't been an easy decision. I've told my peers that I'm gay. I pray that they will not judge me or condemn me. If they ever thought that I was a role model before, I hope they will continue to believe that because I strive to be one. If they thought I was a great schoolteacher before, I hope they will still think the same of me. And for the record, there's a part of me that wants to be a woman."

"It's stereotypes, assumptions and religious ostracism that keep black gay men like me from telling the truth about who we really are. The thought of coming out scared me to death, but now that I've broken my silence, I've never felt happier and prouder of who I am."

"What's your story, narc?" asked the lesbian as Sebastian began French kissing the lad whose hand he was holding.

"Hey... no male-on-male hanky-panky is endorsed in my coffee cottage," shouted Mrs. Drysdale while glaring at Sebastian and his lover. "This isn't The Pink House. I've just about had it with you same-sex skanks. Day in and day out, you all prance into my establishment kidding and chitchatting about meritless LGBT data. Enough is enough. As of this evening, people that promote and facilitate homosexuality are no longer allowed on the premises, effective immediately. Detective Stevenson, can you please do the honors of escorting these FAGS out of my coffee shop? Before I retrieve my sniper rifle and dispatch this feminine fellow to your left and chase these other GAY fellas onto the grounds of that sissy sanctuary that Carla named The Pink House."

"RELAX, Mrs. Drysdale," retorted Sebastian as he stealthily eased toward the counter that separated her from her patrons.

"This old cunt has no right to call us fags," shouted the lad in the tutu as he pulled a hand grenade from the right front pocket of his haversack. "If you were a bit more attractive and a few years younger, I'd remove this cotter pin and manually jam this grenade up your poop chute."

"Hey, is that a real grenade?" asked Loyd as Sebastian sprinted toward Mrs. Drysdale and did a sideways no-hand aerial over the counter that separated them.

"Mind your business, copper," shouted Sebastian's boyfriend while removing his lancet from the canvas sheath affixed to his belt.

"Surely you don't all expect me to stand down while a senior citizen is being chastised and reprimanded," stated Loyd as Sebastian shoved Mrs. Drysdale into a coffee-brewing apparatus.

"Slit her throat, babe," shouted Sebastian's boyfriend.

"Head-butt the nagging hag," shouted the fellow in the tutu.

"It's elderly, incompetent grannies like you that perpetually lobby against same-sex courting," yelled Sebastian while glaring at the now trembling Mrs. Drysdale. "It is elderly, jaded damsels like you that shun the notion of EQUALITY. If Carla were present during that ignorant outburst, she would have gracefully ruptured your spleen and brutally taken away your ability to see and smell. Since our commander-in-chief isn't present and wasn't present, I believe a verbal reprimand will indeed suffice. The fact that you're old enough to be my great-grandmother is primarily why I haven't disunited your spirit from your body. But if I ever hear you say anything negative about the LGBT lifestyle again, I'll abduct your prejudiced son and see to it that he's buried alive with famished flesh-eating beetles."

As Sebastian enlightened Mrs. Drysdale on the dangers of opposing homosexuality, she choked back her signature snarl and smirk. A sense of relief washed over Loyd as it became clear that Sebastian and the others weren't going to dismember Mrs. Drysdale and decimate her java shack.

"I sincerely appreciate you all being merciful this evening," shouted Loyd as he got to his feet. "Mrs. Drysdale is an elderly dame who's the product of an old era. When dealing with biased elders and prejudiced senior citizens, the gay community must simply understand that men and women that were born and raised in the fifties and sixties have been erroneously inculcated with doctrines and theories that are contrary to the new world order. It's been cultivated into their primitive culture to assess all forms of homosexuality as contemptuous conduct and irreverent behavior that needs to be eradicated from the essence of humanity and exterminated from the nucleus of civilization. Mrs. Drysdale is in dire need of enlightenment in matters pertaining to EQUALITY, individualism and same-sex courting. Her forebears and tribal members clearly failed to educate her on the assertion of one's will and personality. It's utterly monumental that openly gay men and women ration out mercy and ample amnesty to people like Mrs. Drysdale."

"Gay marriage is a mockery of natural law," shouted Mrs. Drysdale as she locked eyes with the fellow clutching the hand grenade.

"In fact, homosexual behavior has been observed in more than fifteen hundred species. An Oslo natural history museum created an entire exhibit devoted to "GAY" animals."

"Facts tend to have liberal bias, and for the record Detective Stevenson, I'm well-bred, well-read and shamefully versed in matters that are LGBT related. I've spent countless man-hours researching the evolution and the pandemic of homosexuality. I've got audio footage of Chely Wright proposing to her wife Lauren Blitzer. The two were married in 2011 after the country crooner came out in 2010... I've read the book that Janet Mock wrote entitled *Redefining Realness*. I'm aware, as the land of the free inches toward GAY EQUALITY, hip-hop has been crawling out of its homophobic closet. Amid the slow-moving shift toward tolerance, today's audacious youth may be the loudest voices of reason..."

CHAPTER THIRTY-ONE— BIAS

After watching my fiancé climb into the taxicab, I swaggered into the Willis Tower with my head held high. The corset I had on had my fake boobies sitting up like two armored trucks.

"Hi Carla," whispered a bashful bellboy as I was greeted by a self-conscious gay advocate. The advocate ushered me through several sets of double doors and informed me that there were a slew of journalists and news correspondents impatiently waiting to hear me give a verbal synopsis on my coming out and my transition from male to female.

I entered the boardroom with the grace of a cocky queen that's been seduced and pampered by a thoughtful king.

"Pardon my tardiness," I earnestly stated as I made my way to my designated desk. "As many of you already know, my legal name is Karl Sims. Family, friends, lovers and everyone that understands the law of INDIVIDUALITY address me as Carla. Today, I'd like to give you all a candid digest about my path to womanhood, identity, love and so much more.

"I'm a selfless bitch and a transgender activist. Coming out of the closet allowed me to reach greater inner peace. When I look back at my boyhood, I often say, I always knew I was a dame. Since the age of ten or twelve when I began documenting memories, no one – not my brother, my sister, my lousy mother or my cousins – gave me any reason to believe I was anything other than a rambunctious boy...

"When I say I always knew I was a young lady with such certainty, I nullify all the nuances, the work, the process of self-discovery. I've adapted to saying I always knew I was a girl as a defense against the fickle planet, which has told me that my girlhood was imaginary, something made up that needed to be fixed. I wielded this ever-

155

knowing, all-encompassing certainty to protect my self-esteem and my identity. I've since sacrificed it in an effort to stand firmly in the murkiness of my shifting self-truths.

"I grew to be certain about who I was, but that doesn't mean there wasn't a time when I was learning the world, unsure, unstable, wobbly, dwelling somewhere between confusion, discovery and conviction. The fact that I admit to being uncertain doesn't discount my womanhood. It adds value to it. Though my selfish family in Chicago grew to accept my gender over the years, the same can't be said for my mother, whom I haven't seen in eight years. Despite her absence, I'm still in love with her. As an adolescent diva, I hadn't told my mom I was a girl. I was frightened to do so... She still had an intimidating presence in my life. After a few years of this charade, when I was in my senior year, Mom asked for pictures. I finally sent her my yearbook."

"If your mother was present this very moment, what would you say to her?" asked a female journalist as she adjusted the webcam mount.

"I'd tell her that I'm sorry I haven't spoken to her in years. I'd let her know that I've been going through a lot of shit, things she probably will not approve of and probably wouldn't understand. I'd certainly convey to her how growing up, I always felt different, like I was born in a body that didn't match who I was. Someday in the future I want my mother to realize that the reason I felt different was because I have always been a girl, just in a boy's body. I'm sure she'll be angry with this and won't approve of it.

"I vividly recall when I was growing up, she scolded me for liking Barbie dolls and girlish things, for not playing hockey and lacrosse. I'm sorry that I've disappointed my mom in the past and maybe now, but it's the year 2020 and I'm trying to make myself happy... My mother now knows that I go by Carla now. I don't expect her to approve of this and I know she never will, but I just know my transition is too much for her to process and handle...

"When a person transitions, it doesn't affect only the person undergoing the change, but all those who love that person. I didn't take into account the mourning that my mother and my family would undergo as I evolved... I've been defiantly avoiding all contact and conversation with my mother for years now. I have a lot to tell her, yet I stubbornly tell myself I don't need her approval or love. A piece of me has something to prove to her: despite the years of frustration over who I was, I was a lighthearted and athletic teenage girl and there was shit she could do about it.

"I knew that the physical distance between us kept me safe. The odds of her having the valor to come to the gay community to reprimand me and cuss me out were slim. Several weeks ago I got an email from my mother, which surprised me. In it she complimented me and said my online profile photos "looked nice." She said it would take her awhile to get used to calling me Carla, but she'd try her best.

"Once I'd made the decision to gradually reveal myself, I began alienating myself from those I loved, a decision that made me feel that I was not accountable to anyone. When I look back on the rift between my mother and myself, I realize that I didn't give her the chance I gave my brother, who had time and experience seeing me take all the baby steps I took to unveil myself from lip smackers and tight jeans to name changes and hormone treatments. My mother and I didn't converse when I started hormone treatments. I shunned her calls. Growing up without a mother's validation fueled me to accept, adapt and adore myself."

"Have you undergone the surgical sex change procedure?" asked an elderly fellow as he jotted down notes.

"No... I haven't had the sex change operation yet, for reasons that I'd rather not disclose at this moment. Every now and then I do have pleasant dreams about being groggy in a recovery room with my knees spread apart at a forty-five-degree angle. Those intense dreams about sex operations are stories I intend to someday document in my memoirs. I'm now pleased that my body mirrors me. I'm also pleased with the social media project I've given birth to. The project has given visibility to trans women."

"Are there any women on this planet that inspire you?" asked a CNN correspondent.

"Yes, there are several dozen damsels that inspire me. The chief dame would have to be the stunning Janet Mock. I often marvel at our mutual selflessness."

"People often describe the journey of transsexual people as a passage through the sexes," stated a journalist clutching two laptops, "from manhood to womanhood, from male to female, from boy to girl. That simplifies a complicated journey of self-discovery that goes way beyond gender and genitalia..."

"I concur. My passage was an evolution from bashful boy to glamorous girl. It's been a journey of self-revelation. Undergoing hormone therapy has properly primed me for genital reconstruction surgery. Once I've had the sex change, I'll be sure to share the titillating details with America. Once I've gotten the sex change, I want the gay community, along with the biased naysayers, to understand that I don't battle the maturation of my body merely to get a vagina. I'm in pursuit of something grander than the changing of genitalia. I'm seeking reconciliation with myself..."

"Are you a fan of hip-hop?" asked a columnist cradling a digital camcorder.

"Of course I'm a fan of hip-hop," I candidly stated just as I noticed that one of the male stringers was gazing at me in a way that made me feel pretty and sexy.

"Do you think hip-hop will ever respectfully embrace homosexuality?" asked the lad cradling the camcorder.

"In this time and era the hip-hop culture and the elite entities that are keeping hip-hop alive and relevant have no fucking choice but to respect homosexuality and eventually embrace the LGBT culture. It seems like hip-hop will never respectfully embrace same-sex courting. Even as the gay movement in America progresses, it often feels farfetched. One has to be mindful that in the 90s, when the music biz fixated on unmasking the "gay rapper," or in the early 2000s, when Eminem made a part-time gig out of pissing off gays and "NO HOMO" spread through rap circles like viral vids. As hip-hop evolves, the culture has crept closer to shedding its homophobic armor. Hip-hop had no choice but to embrace extroverted artists like Azealia Banks and Kreayshawn. Lil B endorses loving freely, and Jay-Z, the most eminent MC alive, who once flung "F" bombs "you's the fag model for Karl Kani" granted his most significant endorsement ever – gay marriage – on the heels of President Dotson declaring support.

"Nationally, LGBT (Lesbian, Gay, Bisexual and Transgender) rights are making historic headway. Before Dotson's statement, September

2011 saw the repeal of "Don't Ask, Don't Tell," a divisive 1993 law that banned gay personnel from serving openly in the military."

"Hip-hop owes much of its progress to the brash twenty-five-and-under generation," shouted the stringer that had previously gazed at me in a way that telegraphed his desire to fuck me.

"Those who loathe being labeled embrace androgynous swag and unabashedly gripe with society's old guards. In a move many considered his "coming out," Odd Future's twenty-four-year-old singer/songwriter Frank Ocean published a letter on his Tumblr page on July 4 telling the world his first love was a man. He prefaced his show-and-tell feat with a tweet, expressing "hope that the babies born these days will inherit less of the bullshit than we did." Frank's act caused ripples, but for some from Gen Old, it's a brave new world. Snoop Dogg said in a recent interview, "When I was growing up, you could never do that and announce that. There would be so much scrutiny and hate and negativity. And no one would step FORWARD to support you because that's what we were brainwashed and trained to know."

"Are we all tolerant enough to embrace a gifted gay rapper? Maybe not – non-straight kids still get bullied, and forty-seven percent of Americans are against same-sex marriage. Still, this era's youth are hopeful. Hip-hop pioneers aren't comfortable discussing celebrity coming out parties and the evolution of gay acceptance in hip-hop... The older trailblazers tend to have a hard time embracing the same-sex lifestyle. Fighting against circumstances, openly gay people are often anxious to improve their circumstances... A gay person may be cursed and rich; he or she may be blessed and poor..."

"It's absurd that trans personnel can only serve in eighteen countries, yet not the United States," stated a ruggedly handsome journalist. "I was listening to the Dirty Pop radio station and they were discussing the challenges that transgendered servicemen and women have to face."

"A transition is a lot different than coming out as a lesbian or gay because you're physically changing. I think it's safe to say this generation is the most open-minded. There's more progress since we have access to the Internet and celebrities who will open up. If the president makes a decision to SUPPORT GAY MARRIAGE, you know this generation has come a long way. I find that people automatically think being trans is related to sexuality. It's not. It's gender. And they automatically think, you're trans so you're a gay man. My sexuality and gender are not the same thing."

"Carla, rumors are circulating on social media that you turn into the HULK if you encounter anything that's LGBT-offensive," stated the dame to my left that struck me as being an undercover district attorney.

"If a man, woman or child disrespects the community I'm in, then yes... I do tend to turn into the HULK."

"Jay-Z made a power move by publicly stating his support for gay marriage. How much weight does that support hold in hip-hop?" asked a correspondent that frequently winked at me when his colleagues weren't paying attention.

"To have someone who's the face of hip-hop say something like that is major. Even younger people could respect that. He's a smart man for that. The LGBT community has the most dispensable income. I sometimes think Jay-Z's too old to make a big impact. He's a legend, but that doesn't mean he's popular in the community. Lil Wayne, Drake or Chris Brown need to say that...

"Homophobic males tend to seriously believe that every gay man is interested in them. Many rappers are macho, so it does mean a lot for Jay-Z to say he supports gay marriage. But I think it would've been more powerful for someone like Jay-Z to say, "I was wrong to have been homophobic before, but now I'm in a more secure state of mind and realize that gay people are just as fly, sly and influential as I am...""

"Are you comfortable discussing the portion of misfortune that Chelsea Manning has been given?" asked a young journalist that avoided making eye contact with me.

"I read online that defense secretary Chuck Hagel has approved an army request to transfer national security secrets-leaker Pvt. Chelsea Manning to a civilian federal prison that could provide her treatment to transition to a woman.

"Pentagon officials say that Manning's lawyer blasted the

announcement, saying she'd be less safe in a civilian prison and the transfer is a "strong-arm" attempt to force her into dropping her request for the treatment in a military prison. In a statement, Manning said she didn't request the transfer and was satisfied with a "conservative" treatment plan approved by the army. "The secretary approved a request by army leadership to evaluate potential treatment options for inmates diagnosed with gender dysphoria," Navy Rear Adm. John Kirby, the Pentagon press secretary, said in the statement. The soldier, formerly named Bradley Manning, was convicted of sending classified documents to anti-secrecy website WIKILEAKS. Manning is serving a thirty-five-year prison sentence."

"Do you have a permit to carry that firearm?" asked a Jordanian journalist as he gawked at the revolver that was resting in the holster affixed to my left hip...

CHAPTER THIRTY-TWO— JUDGEMENTAL

"The road to the federal lawsuit was paved shortly after Justin Aaberg's suicide," stated Jessica as her two mastiffs obediently sat at her feet. "When a district teacher contacted the Southern Poverty Law Center to report the anti-gay climate, and the startling proportion of LGBT-related suicide victims. After months of fact-finding, lawyers built a case based on the harrowing stories of anti-gay harassment in order to legally dispute Anoka-Hennepin's neutrality policy. The lawsuit accuses the district of violating the kids' constitutional rights to equal access to education. In addition to making financial demands, the lawsuit seeks to repeal the neutrality policy, implement LGBT sensitivity training for students and staff, and provide guidance for teachers on how to respond to anti-gay bullying."

"The school district hasn't been anxious for a legal brawl," stated George as he began blending sleeping pills into the thirty-six ounces of fine white heroin granules that was being processed for retail distribution. "And the two parties have been in settlement talks practically since the papers were filed. Yet the district still stubbornly clung to the neutrality policy until, at a mid-December school board meeting, it proposed finally eliminating the policy – claiming the move has nothing to do with the discrimination lawsuit – and, bizarrely, replacing it with the controversial topics curriculum policy, which requires teachers to not reveal their personal opinions when discussing CONTROVERSIAL TOPICS.

"The proposal was loudly rejected both by conservatives, who blasted the board for retreating ("The gay activists now have it all," proclaimed one Parents Action League member) and by LGBT advocates, who understood CONTROVERSIAL TOPICS to mean GAYS. Faced with such overwhelming disapproval, the board withdrew its proposed policy in January and suggested a new policy in its place: the Respectful Learning Environment curriculum policy, which the board is expected to swiftly approve."

"The school district insists it has been portrayed unfairly," stated Jessica as the male mastiff playfully gnawed at the bulletproof vest that was left on the floor by one of Jessica's heroin dealers.

"Superintendent Carlson points out it has been working hard to address the mental health needs of its students and hiring more counselors and staff... the policy has created problems for its LGBT community and the instant Carla and her gladiatorial pals get wind of those problems, the Anoka School District will more than likely be decimated and dismantled."

"I understand that gay kids are bullied and harassed on a daily basis, and that can lead to suicide..."

"How could not discussing homosexuality in the public school classrooms cause a teen to take his or her own life?" George asked Jessica. "The notion is absurd. Because homosexual activists have hijacked and exploited teen suicides for their moral and political utility, much of society seems not to be looking closely and openly at all the possible causes of the tragedies, including mental illness. Arguably, however, it is members of the LGBT coalition who have hijacked this entire conversation from the very start: though they've claimed to represent the "MAJORITY" opinion on GAY issues, and say they have thirty-two hundred supporters, one same-sex parent reported that they have more than ten thousand members."

"Carla calls the district's behavior throughout this ordeal IRRATIONAL," stated Jessica as she affectionately petted the female mastiff. "Carla speculates that the district's stupefying denial is a reaction to the terrible notion that they might have played a part in the children's suffering or even their deaths."

"I personally think their minds just reeled in the face of that stress and that horror," shouted George as he poured an ounce of heroin into a digitized cake-mixing blender. "They just lost their way."

"That denial reaches right up to the pinnacle of the local political food chain. President Dotson stayed silent on the suicide cluster for months – until Justin's mom, Tammy Aaberg, forced him to comment. In September, while Dotson was running for the presidential nomination, Aaberg delivered a petition of one hundred forty-one thousand signatures to Dotson's campaign headquarters, asking him to address the Anoka-Hennepin suicides and publicly denounce ANTI-GAY bullying. Dotson has publicly stated his opposition to anti-bullying legislation, asking in a state senate committee hearing, "What will be our definition of bullying? Will it get to the point where we are completely stifling free speech and expression? Will we be expecting boys to be girls?" Dotson responded to the petition with a generic letter to constituents, telling them that, "bullying is wrong" and "all human lives have undeniable value." Tammy Aaberg found out about the letter secondhand.

"Tammy's suffering hasn't ended. In mid-December, her nine-year-old son was hospitalized for suicidal tendencies. He tried to drown himself in the bathtub, wanting to see his big brother again... Justin's suicide has put Tammy on a mission, transforming her into an LGBT activist and a den mother for gay teens, intent upon turning her own tragedy into others' salvation. She knows too well the price of indifference, or hostility, or denial. Because there's one group of kids who can't afford to live in denial, a group for whom the usual raw teenage struggles over identity, peer acceptance and controlling one's own impulsivity are matters of extreme urgency – quite possibly matters of life or death."

"I'm willing to bet my last dollar that the SKANK Carla has no idea that Anoka Middle School for the Arts recently held their first GAY-STRAIGHT Alliance meeting of the school year," shouted Jessica after giving two of her heroin merchants the green light to start packaging the dope. "She's probably on the top floor barking orders at her eccentric comrades as she gives that homicide detective another exclusive tour of the command center. That bloody Pink House has been a crucial place for LGBT kids and their friends to find support and learn coping skills and combat skills. There are now eighty-eight to one hundred twenty-one openly gay people always stationed outside of The Pink House. Many of them are armed and dangerous. I've heard same-sex couples gush about how affirming the club is – and how necessary..."

"I like Carla," shouted George after pouring twenty-eight grams of heroin into a plastic chalice. "She's a woman of focus, a woman of taste and sophistication. She's a queen in demeanor and a queen in thought. I've read tweets that stated she's a bitch that's twice as consistent as the ants and just as productive and constructive as a honeybee..."

"Don't exalt that harlot in my presence," shouted Jessica. "She flaunts her sexual orientation and that alone is why I've been entertaining the thought of dethroning her and having her relinquish all the power, capital and influence she has over to me."

"Relax, boss lady. I'll make a few calls and see if I can facilitate the dethronement of Carla. My street instinct tells me that the crown she wears belongs on top of your head..."

"You haven't got the wit, nor the resources, to facilitate such a power move."

"I've got connections," shouted the merchant. "I can have Carla dispatched and dethroned."

"You're a boy," shouted Jessica. "A boy that enjoys packaging heroin and peddling heroin. You couldn't dispatch Carla if I ordered you to, and you sure as hell couldn't have her dethroned, even if I paid you."

As Jessica ranted about how the heroin merchant wasn't astute enough to dethrone and dispatch Carla, the merchant began to think about Catilina, a damsel that he knew could and would dethrone Carla, dispatch her, and hand-deliver her entrails if he requested. He also knew that Catilina would want at least a million dollars wired to her offshore account to carry out the assassination...

CHAPTER THIRTY-THREE— INDIVIDUALITY

As an openly gay boy vainly cried out for help, the school board was busy trying to figure out how to continue tactfully ignoring the existence of LGBT boys like him. Justin Aaberg's suicide had sent the district into damage control mode. They feared an expected visit from the Defenders of Same-Sex Courtship. The district knew that Carla and the Defenders would offer perpetual protection and solace to gay students in crisis.

LGBT students were stunned to be told for the first time about the existence of the neutrality policy that had been responsible for their teachers' behavior, but no one was more outraged to hear of it than Tammy Aaberg. Six weeks after her son's death, Aaberg became the first to publicly confront the Anoka-Hennepin School Board about the link between the policy, ANTI-GAY bullying and suicide. She demanded that the policy be revoked.

"What about my parents' rights to have my gay son go to school and learn without being bullied?" Aaberg asked, weeping as the board stared back impassively from behind a raised dais.

Anti-gay backlash was instant. Minnesota Family Council President Tom Princhard blogged that Justin's suicide could only be blamed upon one thing: "HIS GAYNESS."

"Youth who embrace homosexuality are at greater risk of suicide, because they've embraced an unhealthy sexual identity and lifestyle," Prichard wrote. Rumor has it that Carla allegedly had him kidnapped, castrated and fed his own foreskin... Anoka-Hennepin conservatives formally organized into the Parents Action League, declaring opposition to the "RADICAL Homosexual" agenda in schools. Its stated goals, advertised on its website, included promoting Day of Truth, providing resources for students "seeking to leave the homosexual lifestyle," supporting the neutrality policy and targeting "PRO-GAY activist teachers who fail to abide by district policies." Asked on a radio program whether the anti-gay agenda of her ilk bore any responsibility for the bullying and suicides, the cowardly creep and co-author of the original "NO HOMO PROMO" held fast to her principles, blaming pro-gay groups for the tragedies. She explained that such "child corruption" agencies allow "gay kids to wrongly feel legitimized" and then these kids are locked into a lifestyle with their choices limited, and many times this can be disastrous to them as they get into behavior that leads to disease...

The co-author of the original NO HOMO PROMO was reportedly found bound to a garbage truck with her spine ruptured. The medical examiner told E News that a total of thirteen porcupine quills had to be surgically extracted from her vulva and vaginal region. Although Carla was noted for being solely responsible for the woeful act, no charges were ever filed...

The co-author added that if LGBT kids weren't encouraged to come out of the closet in the first place, they wouldn't be bullied. Yet, while everyone in the district was buzzing about the neutrality policy, the board simply refused to discuss it, not even when students began appearing before them to detail their experiences with LGBT harassment. The board stated quite clearly that they were standing behind that policy and were not willing to take another look, further insulating itself from reality. The district launched an investigation into the suicides and, unsurprisingly, absolved itself of any responsibility...

"Based on all of the information we've been able to gather," read a statement from the superintendent's office, "none of the suicides were connected to incidents of bullying or harassment."

Just to be on the safe side, however, the district held Power Point presentations in a handful of schools to train teachers in how to defend gay students from harassment while also remaining neutral on homosexuality. One slide instructed teachers that if they heard gay slurs, the best response would be a tepid "that language is unacceptable in this school." (If a more authoritative response was needed, the slide added, the teacher could continue with the stilted, almost apologetic explanation, "In this school we are required to welcome all people and to make them feel safe.") But teachers were, of course, reminded to never show "personal support for LGBT people" in the classroom.

Teachers left the training sessions more confused than ever about how to interpret the rules. And the board, it turned out, was equally confused. When a local advocacy group, GAY EQUITY TEAM, met with the school board, the vice-chair thought the policy applied only to health classes, while the chair asserted it applied to all curricula. And when the district legal council commented that some discussions about homosexuality were allowed, yet another board member expressed surprise, saying he thought any discussion on the topic was forbidden. "How can the district ever train on a policy that they do not understand themselves...?" The board is confused! With the adults thus distracted by endless policy discussion, the entire district became a place of dread for gay students...

CHAPTER THIRTY-FOUR— AMOROUS...

As a late afternoon storm beats against the windows, the stunning yet vicious Catilina Ortega sits in her living room. Her layered auburn hair falls into her face. Her ears are lined with piercings. Her nail polish is black. On the table before her are six photos: one of charitable Carla, one of warmhearted Walter, one of helpful Heather, a wallet-size photo of solicitous Sharon, another wallet-size photo of kindhearted Kevin. A photo of benevolent Devin was also among the pictures. To the left of the six photographs sat two Uzis and a black ski mask. To the right of Catilina stood two agile assassins that exuded aggression. Both men were sly veterans in the killing profession. The Remington rifles they were clutching belonged to Catilina. The pistols resting in their shoulder holsters were their personal side arms. The men weren't alarmed at all to see the curvaceous Catilina covered in blood.

"Would you like me to run you some bathwater?" asked Larry after placing the Remington rifle on the eighteenth-century English settee.

"Yes," stated Catilina, "a hot bubble bath would suffice. I may as well shit, shave and bathe before we murder Carla and launch her five flunkies..."

"Will Larry and I be awarded the sacred opportunity to bathe you again?" asked Donnie as he unfastened his trousers.

"I'd love for you two to bathe me again," whispered Catilina while removing her bloody blouse. "I'm feeling frisky and slutty this evening. Therefore, I may just allow you and Larry to orally please me while I devise Carla's demise."

Eight minutes later, Catilina and the two assassins were submersing themselves in the bubble-filled bathtub. All three parties were nude and stoic. The mane between Catilina's legs was in need of a major grooming. The platinum trinket that dangled from her pierced bellybutton wasn't as opulent as the pearl-studded trinket that dangled from her pierced clitoris.

The water was hot and soapy, just as Catilina preferred it. The lights were turned down low. Several jasmine-scented candles were lit. The voice of Janelle Monáe was streaming out of the concealed Clarion speakers. Larry had a slight erection. Donnie was lathering up three sponges...

"You're beautiful!" whispered Larry as he gazed into Catilina's eyes.

"Am I more beautiful than Carla?"

"Carla's attractive... she isn't at all beautiful," shouted Larry as Donnie handed him a soap sponge.

"Would you fuck her?" asked Catilina as Donnie began washing her left foot.

"I'd fuck her," shouted Donnie as Larry began washing her upper back.

"You'd fuck anything that has a pulse and a nice bust," shouted Catilina.

"Yes... yes, I'd fuck Carla. Who wouldn't fuck a transsexual that used embezzled cash to refurbish, revitalize and upgrade the tombstones that belong to Rosa Parks, Coretta Scott King, Harriet Tubman and Joan Rivers? I find it appalling that we've been activated to sink her battleship. Murdering a damsel like Carla will surely disenchant the gods, gratify Lucifer, taunt karma and cast a hex over us and our future offspring..."

"Gibberish," Catilina chimed in as Donnie began scrubbing the heel of her right foot. "Dispatching homosexuals is a profession that inner-city hoodlums and bluebloods adore, endorse and often idolize. The slimy aristocrats in Germany and Spain are infamously known for constructing copper statues of the men and women that dismember and disembowel gay advocates, gay couples and same-sex newlyweds. Although hunting LGBT members is not particularly my forte, the bounty that's been placed on Carla and her companions is a bounty that'll secure our future indefinitely."

"It baffles me that a member of Jessica's heroin-selling squadron would be willing to pay us one million dollars to assassinate Carla and five of her closest affiliates," stated Larry as he began scrubbing Catilina's lower back. "Carla's an accomplished diva. She's also the editor-in-chief of a monumental newspaper called *Black and Pink*."

"*Black and Pink*, huh?"

"Does the paper divulge data about the operational blueprint of The Pink House?" asked Catilina as Donnie ran his left thumb across her now hardened right nipple.

"The paper doesn't disclose much intel about The Pink House," stated Larry. "The paper was designed to help heterosexuals understand transgender diversity. The paper discloses a sensible explanation of sexual and gender identities. It's a well-written, perfectly organized and easily comprehensible newspaper. Though the text is primarily focused on issues facing trans people, it is also a manual for the general understanding of human diversity and personal individuality as well. Carla's witty and humorous personality shines through the pages of the newspaper as she educates and informs people of many serious issues facing our society as a whole, and especially the gay community. The newspaper is literally a reference manual for those considering a transition, who are in transition, or who would simply like to dispel their ignorance of what being openly gay is and the struggles caused by the fear and ignorance experienced by the homosexuals of the world..."

"I love the newspaper for the wisdom it contains," shouted Donnie after planting several wet kisses behind Catilina's right ear.

"The paper talks a lot about EQUALITY. First let me say, there is a lot of same-sex marriage information in the newspaper, one hundred fourteen pages. I spent a lot of time on the phone talking about it with my cousin, browsing the Internet and downloading more information. Next, let me say I recommend that you, Jessica, and all of your heroin dealers read it. It's informative to the goals of the Black and Pink Family. Their website is www.againstEQUALITY.org."

"I've visited that website," shouted Catilina as Donnie began kissing her toes. "It's an online archive, publishing and arts collective focused on critiquing mainstream gay and lesbian politics. As queer thinkers, writers and artists, they are committed to dislodging the centrality of equality rhetoric and challenging the demand for inclusion in the institution of marriage, the US military, and the prison industrial complex via hate crime legislation."

"It sounds like the bitch Carla is trying to reinvigorate the queer political imagination," shouted Larry as he began easing his index finger into Catilina's hairy pussy...

CHAPTER THIRTY-FIVE— HYPOCRISY

"I despise damsels that sleep with men that support segregating others by ethnicity, nationality, religion and SEXUAL IDENTITY," shouted Heather as she entered the den.

"I've got a question! Do you ever see police stopping and frisking white middle class and upper class homosexuals?" asked Sharon as she sashayed into the den, clutching a strawberry popsicle.

"NO..." retorted Heather, "they go to the inner city and the poor areas, determine them to be high crime areas, and use that as an excuse to violate search and seizure protections guaranteed to openly gay citizens in the Constitution. The government is a corporate entity, a corporate entity that often feels ashamed and threatened by the rise and reign of LGBT... History tells us that those that are openly gay and least able to protect themselves are the targets of the greatest oppression..."

"Why don't they harass the homosexuals in Boys Town and West Hollywood? Is there less crime there? It's the year 2020 – statistics tell us that the crimes committed by whites, blacks, heterosexuals, homosexuals and other racial minorities are about the same throughout the nation's population. As a white female who grew up in a suburban setting, I can attest that drug use and homosexuality rates were as high or higher than that of my friends in the city schools... But what cop is going to take the chance of harassing a state representative's gay kid, or a lawyer's gay kid...? Yet they go to the city and they harass gay people, usually homosexuals of color... Hundreds upon hundreds are bullied and harassed daily. Carla and the others are fed up with LGBT members being targeted by the cops. In our last meeting, Carla's cabinet made it quite clear that cops that target LGBT members will now be targeted."

"I'd love to tackle a deputy that opposes same-sex adoption," shouted Sharon as she began undressing. "I'd cloak the cop in hot tar and white cotton and hang him from the sycamore tree that's in our vineyard..."

"Eighty to ninety percent of the homosexuals that are harassed by cops are flamboyant, voguish and harmless. I'd like to point out that violence against LGBT members is the most pandemic form of violence in the world."

"I agree," stated Heather as she removed her strapless bra. "In our next meeting I'm gonna propose that we install a hotline at The Pink House that LGBTQ people in prison can call to connect with volunteers who can provide supportive listening and resource referrals."

"That's an innovative idea," shouted Sharon as she removed her panties. "I'll be sure to remind you to run that idea by Carla and the cabinet."

"What idea?" asked Walter as he sauntered into the den carrying a box full of plastic coat hangers.

"She thinks it'll be a splendid idea to install a hotline at The Pink House that's outfitted to accept calls from LGBT prisoners," stated Sharon while extracting a cigar from the glass case.

"It's obvious that Carla and Loyd will support that idea," stated Walter. "Why are you two always conversing in the nude?"

"Why are you always rearranging Carla's closet without her consent?" Heather retorted.

"Hey, those shorts you're wearing sure do look familiar..." Sharon chimed in as she scrutinized the skin-tight boy shorts that Walter was wearing.

"I enjoy organizing the commander's closet," shouted Walter as Sharon lit the hand-rolled cigar she was clutching. "You two harlots need to shave and bathe because it smells like fish and corn chips in here."

"Quit hating, Walter. Carla has reprimanded you twice already for hating on us," Heather retorted. "And I assure you that this den doesn't smell of chips and fish. That pleasant scent that greeted you when you pranced into this den was the priceless redolence of unspoiled, well-maintained adult pussy."

"Virginal pussy," Sharon chimed in. "Pussy that's wet, warm, edible and prone to squiring cum onto the methodical tongue of a liberal lesbian..."

"What's going on in here?" asked Devin as he swaggered into the den cradling a crate filled with hand grenades and upscale Bowie knives.

"I was just telling Heather and Sharon that it smells like seafood and corn chips in here," shouted Walter while grinning like a witty comedian.

"And we were just telling Walter that the scent he's failed to identify is nothing more than unblemished pussy that's never encountered a stiff dick or a gentleman's tongue..."

"While you ladies are up here bantering, Kevin and I are ready to brief the squadron on this week and next week's itinerary."

"Hey, don't blow that cigar smoke in my face," shouted Walter as he was exiting the den.

"Where's Carla?" asked Sharon as she blew smoke rings at Heather.

"She called a few minutes ago," Devin reported. "Her chauffeur was scheduled to pick her up ten minutes ago from the novelty store adjacent to the Willis Tower.

CHAPTER THIRTY-SIX— TRANSJUSTICE

A quick glance at my onyx-encrusted timepiece confirmed that my comely, complacent chauffeur was once again tardy. By the time he pulled up in front of the novelty store, I'd already decided that he wasn't fit or punctual enough to be my hired driver.

"Pardon my tardiness, mistress," shouted the incompetent chauffeur as he exited the Rolls Royce Phantom and rushed over to open the rear door for me.

"You're fired, James!" I sternly stated as I sashayed past the groveling driver and made a beeline for the driver's seat. "As of this very second, your services are no longer needed or valued. Eighty-six seconds ago I deemed you a liability, a hindrance when it comes to facilitating my movements to and fro."

"You can't fire me!" shouted the tardy driver as I climbed behind the wheel of the sedan.

"I just did," I firmly stated while shutting the driver-side door.

"You're a bitch!" yelled the chauffeur as I adjusted the driver's seat and readjusted the rearview mirror.

"I'm the same bitch that paid your daughter's college tuition, you ungrateful parasite. The same bitch that helped you pay off your mortgage and pay for your boyfriend's chemotherapy."

Before the parasitic driver could reply, I eased the gearshift into drive and swerved into the downtown rush hour traffic. Several car horns honked and blared as I damn near sideswiped a 2012 Lotus Evora. While traveling east down Lakeshore Drive, it began to dawn on me that same-sex courting would always be prohibited in certain states and countries, yet permitted in a few countries and states. For years now, I've been trying to understand what's so taboo about same-sex marriage and why people deem same-sex adoption deplorable and flagrant...

As tears of confusion compromised my eye shadow and false lashes, I heard the still small voice within me speak: "Americans will never ever uphold EQUALITY," stated the voice in my head as a state trooper zipped past me. "Americans are naturally biased, judgmental and hypocritical. America as a country lacks motivation, readiness or the strength it takes to recognize homosexuality as a divine culture that gives planet Earth character and grandeur..."

Eight minutes later I was pulling into the parking lot that belonged to the Chinese bistro. As I allowed my whiskey-colored Rolls Royce Phantom to parallel park itself, I thought about the one man that makes me feel special and relevant...

Thoughts about my soon-to-be husband were rudely quieted the moment I spotted an aspiring mobster dressed to the hilt in Ferragamo apparel, clutching a poorly manufactured picket sign. The anti-gay insignia that was printed on the picket sign not only ruffled my feathers, but it also sent chills up my spine.

I smoothly exited the Phantom...

CHAPTER THIRTY-SEVEN— CAPTIOUS...

Tony's father, Mr. Drysdale, was standing on the street corner wielding a picket sign, yelling gay slurs at a gay couple that walked past holding hands. His critical cohorts were also wielding picket signs and yelling homophobic slurs at openly gay pedestrians. Mr. Drysdale and his cohorts gawked at the sleek Rolls Royce as it pulled into the parking lot and parallel parked next to a '61 Cadillac.

"She's stunning," shouted Tony's father after Carla exited the Phantom.

"She's sexy as hell," the chap to his left clutching a picket sign chimed in, just as Carla was adjusting her corset and her shoulder holster.

"She's armed and voluptuous," shouted Mr. Drysdale as Carla abruptly removed her Gianvito Rossi peep toe pumps.

"She's headed our way," stated a young lady, also wielding a picket sign.

As Carla sashayed over to Tony's dad, the other picketers marveled at her physique and bewitching mystique. The second she stepped within arm's reach of Mr. Drysdale, she abruptly snatched the picket sign from him and snapped the sign into several fragments.

As Mr. Drysdale glared at Carla, she administered a deadly kick to his sternum. Seconds after the kick was administered, he started hacking up mucus and blood, an official sign that she'd ruptured his spleen and splintered four ribs.

As Tony's dad fell to the flagstone pavement, Carla approached the picketer to her right. After closing the gap between them, she sternly instructed the fellow to hand her the picket sign he was clutching. As the lad made an admirable effort to hand Carla the sign, she head-butted the man and he too fell to the flagstone pavement. His high-pitched screaming assured Carla that she had damaged his palate and that the fellow would surely need oral surgery. Carla was pleased that she sent her forehead crashing into the man's mouth. She felt his two front incisors had pierced her forehead. Blood trickled down her face as she straightened out her wig.

After adjusting her wig, she sashayed over to her armored Rolls Royce. Before climbing into the Phantom, she retrieved her designer pumps from the curb. Now seated in the driver's seat, she pushed a digitized button and the Rolls Royce was resurrected. The sound of police sirens could be heard in the distance as Carla swerved across oncoming traffic and back as she regained control of the car

Thirty-eight minutes later she was pulling onto her cobblestone driveway.

CHAPTER THIRTY-EIGHT— CLASH OF THE SEXES...

The stunning drag queen that stormed out of The Pink House was clutching an eight-inch Howitzer. The self-propelled Howitzer was capable of firing a two-hundred-pound projectile sixteen thousand eight hundred meters. Just as the drag queen raised the weapon to fire at the National Guard troops, she was struck in the chest and abdominal region. The bullet that pierced her chest ended her life on impact. The Cook County sheriff responsible for taking her life was clutching a CAR-15, a carbine version of the M-16. After the armed drag queen was killed, a transgendered titan cloaked in full body armor stepped forward and shot the sheriff in the face. The gunfight between the heterosexuals and the homosexuals was in full swing. Both parties were now guilty of at least one brutal massacre. The shootout went on for what seemed like a time-warped forty-eight and a half minutes, which made the senses of those involved feel like it had lasted for four and a half hours.

The street and sidewalks were now littered with corpses and critically injured human beings. Shell casings of all kinds also peppered the sidewalk and intersection. National Guard soldiers were crouched behind SWAT utility vehicles, trying to resuscitate their wounded brothers. Same-sex sentinels were crouched behind their luxury sedans, reloading their weapons and having a brief moment of silence for their fallen LGBT tribal members.

Cook County sheriffs and Lake County sheriffs were fleeing the mayhem on foot while barking orders and numerical codes at the fire and rescue dispatcher. Local beat cops and the Gang Task Force Unit were cowering behind unmarked squad cars, news vans and armored SUVs...

Media personnel and K-9 officers were frantically crawling underneath cars, buses and vans...

Transgendered teens and bisexual boys were coughing up blood and clawing at the asphalt as dauntless lesbians ushered them to safety...

Homicide detectives and rookie cops were laying face down in puddles of their own blood and brain matter. Weapons of every make and model lined the street and sidewalk. Empty machine guns and blood-covered swords were seen lying next to the deceased homosexuals. Shrapnel from assorted grenades and fully functional sniper rifles was scattered between dying heterosexuals. A dozen or so police units were set on fire during the orchestrated massacre. So were several state troopers.

Eight deputized K-9s were put down and quite a few media correspondents were severely injured. Riot shields, pepper spray canisters, billy clubs and handheld two-way walkie-talkies were also scattered among perishing patrolmen. Shell fragments from highly explosive shells, along with crossbows, were everywhere.

Narcs and DEA agents stumbled into burning police cruisers and snazzy sedans while trying to manually extract arrows from their torsos and limbs. Twenty or so US marshals along with six FBI agents were grappling with ten or so brawny transsexuals and several openly gay mobsters. While they engaged in hand-to-hand combat, the police commissioner was climbing into his modified SUV. The bullet that had entered his buttock was a .357 round. As he climbed into the modified municipal SUV, he could hear deputies screaming in horror and wounded homosexuals shrieking in terror.

The blaring horns from approaching fire trucks, along with the emergency sirens from approaching EMT vehicles, could be heard clearly. News choppers and other municipal helicopters circled overhead as military drones gracefully hovered over the horrific scene. Recording video footage and audio footage of the savage and indiscriminate wholesale killings, the drones were armed and also had a panoramic view over the madness that had just unfolded in front of The Pink House.

As the drones uploaded video and audio footage, an AH-1G attack helicopter was landing on the roof of The Pink House. The damsel at the helm of the AH-1G was Carla's first sergeant. She was in charge of the mechanical and operational wellbeing of the aircraft. She was volatile, yet had a refined feel for the controls of the chopper. In the chopper with her was a warrant officer who endorsed gay marriage and same-sex adoption. In the cabin of the helicopter were crates of ammunition and explosives.

Also landing on the roof were two medical evacuation helicopters. The pilot was a bisexual brute. The flak vest he had on was a heavy vest designed to stop shrapnel. The aircraft commander was a transgendered male. On his lap sat an AK-47. The 7.62 mm automatic rifle belonged to Sebastian.

Unbeknownst to the aircraft commander, Sebastian had perished two minutes and twenty-eight seconds ago... The crate of C-4 that was sitting on the floor was primed for detonation... On the roof of The Pink House, lying face down in a pool of their own blood and urine were three poorly trained Navy SEALs who opposed same-sex parenting. One of the SEALs had a bayonet stuck in his mouth. Beside him rested an M-79. The 40 mm single-shot break-open grenade launcher looked like a sawed-off shotgun with a fat barrel. To the left lay the other two SEAL Team operatives. Both men's corpses were riddled with bullets. Next to the two deceased SEALs were an M-16 and an M-60. The M-60 was a standard US light machine gun, 7.62 mm. The M-16 was a standard infantry rifle. Standing over them was an openly gay Olympic hopeful. In his right hand was a rifle that was missing its detachable blade. The grin on his face and the tears in his eyes assured the occupants of both choppers that the lad standing over the three corpses was a Defender of Same-Sex Courtship.

Inside The Pink House on the eighth floor stood eight blue-blooded bisexuals. Each man was clutching a flamethrower. They were given the task of securing the eighth floor by all available means.

The eight blue-blooded bisexuals had no idea that approximately six hundred seventy-six same-sex avengers were sprawled out in front of their headquarters, pulseless. They also had no idea that a little over nine hundred law enforcement officials were also sprawled out in front of The Pink House with either their throats slit or their bodies peppered with projectiles, arrows and foreign shrapnel...

The uninjured Defenders of Same-Sex Courtship were reloading their weapons and priming themselves for round two...

The armed and unharmed law enforcement personnel were reloading their weapons and hoping to God the valorous Defenders didn't initiate round two.

Defenders of Same-Sex Courtship

Dear Reader,

If you're lusting to find out what happens to Carla, Loyd and the remaining Defenders of Same-Sex Courtship, you must tune in to read Volume Two.

Volume Two will be available online later this year. I ask and pray that you follow Carla on her quest to promote and facilitate the uplift of EQUALITY and homosexuality.

Hugs and white roses to every heterosexual and homosexual that took time out of their day to read, review, assess, critique and scrutinize this epic tale.

--Abdul Robinson

ABOUT THE AUTHOR

ABDUL ROBINSON is a thirty-four-year-old former inner-city hoodlum that's evolved into a prince of a man. He's the father of two sons. He's a motherless man that's also a fatherless father. His primary objective while on Earth is to strategically put himself in a position to feed, cloth, and shelter four hundred eighty thousand orphans.

Although currently smothered in chains and shackles, Abdul is what we diplomats like to call an ebony-colored phoenix that's attempting to emerge from the ashes. His transformation is astoundingly miraculous. He's somehow vanquished his former pirate-like ways. Sincerity can now be smelled on his breath. Being quarantined from society has amplified his now incorruptible perception. He now conducts himself like an authentic knight that's high-principled, and utterly trustworthy...

His perspective on manhood and fatherhood is no longer flawed and jaded. He's sound, sober and spiritually balanced. Abdul is a king that's queen less and crownless. He's the epitome of a rehabilitated prisoner. His writing in regards to creativity is without question ultra-innovative. He has a writer's spirit, and the imagination of an educated wizard. He's what my wife calls a rose that's growing out of the concrete. He's a phenomenal storyteller, yet he doesn't even know it. Most collegiate writers would declare him as being illegally creative, and that his level of creativity should be unconstitutionally outlawed and banned from display.

Sincerely spoken by

DEANDRE ROBINSON

References

Erdely, Sabrina Rubin. "School." *Rolling Stone* 16 Feb. 2012: 49-68. Print.

"Diversity In Civil Rights Leadership: This Is The New Naacp." *Jet Magazine*. Print.

"Mich. Judge Stikes Down State's Gay-Marriage Ban." *Usa Today*. Print.

"Hagel Oks Transferring Manning To Civilian Prison." *Usa Today*. Print.

Thomas R., Chandra. "To My Beautiful Black Sisters." *Essence* Jul. 2011. Print.
"Details." *Essence*. Oct. 2011: 121. Print.

"In Box: Open Arms." *Essence*. Oct. 2013: 28. Print.

Morrison, Veronica. "Mailbag: Transgender Marriage." *People* 3 June 2013: 6. Print.

"Diana The Great." *Essence* Sept. 2011: 187. Print.

Garraud, Tracy. Tyutyunik, Misha. "Generation Sex." *Vibe* 15 Oct. 2012. Print.

"Where There's Gay Marriage Comes...The Rise Of Gay Divorce." *Essence* Oct. 2011. Print.

www.ingramcontent.com/pod-product-compliance
Lightning Source LLC
Chambersburg PA
CBHW031337170626
46807CB00002B/741